Grunge Rock Alien

Cronos Carpio

Published by Cronos Carpio, 2024.

GRUNGE ROCK ALIEN

First edition. July 19, 2024.

Copyright © 2024 Cronos Carpio.

ISBN: 979-8227867780

Written by Cronos Carpio.

This book is dedicated to the memory of my dear friend, Gustavo Adolfo Chacón Vargas. May you rest in peace, brother. Hope you can still hear the music that inspired us both. The Grunge songs and Grunge Gods to whom I also pay tribute to.

DISCLAIMER

The following book is a satire on Woke Culture. Its comments and criticism are proposed as a parody of the overindulgences of the Crystal Generation. In no way is the content intended to inspire hate and negativity towards zoomers, celebrities, minorities, Little People, Vegans, bipolar disorder and mental illness, terrorism, suicide and rape victims, women and feminism, the Hispanic community, the Pro-life and Pro-choice stand on abortion, the Black Lives Matter movement, drug abuse and users, republican or liberal ideals, the Jewish, Muslim and Christian faith, overweight and obese people, Southern Americans, LGBTQA+ identities and musical genres overall. Reader discretion and accountability is advised.

Copyright Disclaimer under section 107 of the Copyright Act of 1976, allowance is made for "fair use" for purposes such as criticism, comment, news reporting, teaching, scholarship, education and research. Authentic name brands have been treated fairly and accurately as a positive tribute to the city of Seattle, Washington. All copyrighted references have been properly credited in the bibliography found in the PDF version and the link at the end of the book.

GROUND ZERO

After what felt like an eternal slumber, the teenager Vic Grunge woke up in a strange spaceship surrounded by four outdated cassette tapes. At its center there was another artifact with headphones labeled *Walkman*. His wardrobe was entirely shady; grey T-shirt, dusky ripped jeans and black Converse shoes. He had absolutely no recollection about his whereabouts nor his past. In fact, he didn't even remember who he was, what he was or that his name was Vic Grunge.

His confusion and disorientation only altered him more. Especially the round hole in his chest that contained a strange liquid of fluorescent characteristics. One which appeared to boil when feeling uneasy like he did in that precise moment. But the answer was right in front of him the whole time. A blinking red light alongside a VHS tape with a sticker showing the words "PLAY ME" in pink crayon.

Vic got up and picked up the VHS tape. He examined the switchboard and noticed there was a slot of the same proportions below a large television. The videotape was introduced in the slot and the red light stopped blinking. This last action turned on the screen which immediately played the tape. A much older man that himself appeared on the TV. He was wearing a black flannel shirt, had long silver hair and appeared to be very sick. His eyes were fixated directly on the camera that videotaped him with somewhat poor quality. The man in the flannel shirt began to speak as though he knew every aspect of his life. And there was a perfectly good reason why:

Hello. You probably have many questions right about now. Starting with your origins, your identity and your beliefs. Also, the spaceship that brought you to your current destination. Which is not your home planet, by the way. This last one is called Earth. Well... was called really. Human beings were very smart in many ways but very stupid in others. I'll focus on the stupidity which is the part that concerns your present dilemma.

Basically, we failed as a species. And only because we thought we were winners. It was Pride that led us to extinction. Everybody started to think that they were better than the rest because of their close-minded beliefs. This was meant for peace and equality, but eventually, turned into nuclear warfare. And not between Nations but between the people themselves. Spawning from the nuclear availability in the future to increase our technological capabilities.

I am your father. My name is Vincent and your name is Victor Grunge. Your last name was crafted by myself and your mother Hanna based on our love for Grunge music. Some of it contained in the four cassette tapes that you have in your possession. This will be your medicine. As you are sick in a very special way.

Both your mother and myself suffer from Bipolar Disorder. I'm afraid you have it as well. You'll feel very sad and very happy from time to time. You also have rapid cycling so it will happen more often than a regular Bipolar. But the dangerous part comes from your chest. When the nuclear riots were at their peak, radiation levels started escalating to biblical proportions. Everyone, including pacifists who took no part in the madness, started to die. I was a chemist, a nuclear engineer, a geneticist and an astrophysicist. With my knowledge, I managed to solve the puzzle to keep us from becoming extinct. But my time was limited and I only had time to save one of us. We chose you. Hence the hole in your chest.

The plutonium was installed in a nuclear reactor in your torso which made you invulnerable to the radiation spewed by humanity. Though it kept you safe, it came at a price. Not only will you be incapable of removing it, but any profound alteration in your Bipolar mood can set it off and kill you and everybody on the planet instantly. Same goes for dying by any other means. So, the first and most important rule is, never get too sad or too happy. Protect yourself and fight all your suicidal urges. How do you keep this in check? Listen to Grunge when you're feeling down. Listen to Grunge when you're feeling euphoric. It's the only way. It won't stop all the pain nor will it be full proof to contain the explosion, but it's the best option I can offer you given the lack of meds in our current Apocalypse.

You probably think I did everything to get you where you are. But I didn't. You were already 13 years old at the time and were always very bright. Incredibly mature for your age. I knew my time was up, but you insisted that I taped myself with the explanation since you would suffer from temporary amnesia on your journey due to the nebular interference in between both worlds. And even though you'll start remembering everything very quickly, it would be more believable for you this way. Though my technology at the time was far superior, we decided to use retro tech so you could always remember the 90s. A period you actually belonged to. Though of an older age, your clothes and your Walkman have been treated to withstand extreme elemental conditions. As an astrophysicist, I discovered a new planet. It would take you 5 years in the spaceship you helped me build to reach it. Which means you'll be eighteen when you get there.

I managed to establish contact with the residents of that planet. It's called Window World and people are made up of glass. I picked them because they're sensitive and already agreed to receiving you in the four Crystal Cities. Something that might be beneficial to your nuclear Bipolar state. Except for the fact they'll reach Generation Z or zoomer status upon your arrival. Meaning they'll be extremely PC. So be careful. Their world is much more different than Earth.

It's square instead of round. Like the name implies, it's a vertical window in space. Which means it's not even a cube as ours was a sphere. It has a yellow sun Solar System, but both the planet's rotation and revolution happen to be much faster.

If you followed my instructions, you should be now in Ground Zero. The center of the planet. A dead zone really. You can live there or go to any of the Crystal Cities through the four perpendicular roads. It's extremely small in comparison to Earth. You'll find each entrance at walking distance and the whole planet is made up of these four cities.

The second rule is that you must respect their customs. Remember that you are the alien there. Being zoomers, they might not take kindly to any opposition you give them. Learn to walk among them. You'll meet four human clones and will have access to magical flannel shirts. Both personally engineered by me to help you on your quest. At the end of each section, you will also be visited by the Alternative Valkyrie. A holy idol to whom you may confess all your darkest thoughts to further be absolved from them.

As for Window World, note they have taken many of my suggestions. Including the English language, human history, human religion, human music, human sports and the city design which resembles the city of Seattle. They even terraformed the Washington nature and climate using my clone tech. You'll realize you were not raised there but it will help you maintain our Grunge origins. Your coming has been viewed with divine hope. But it doesn't mean it will be easy. Try to perpetuate our message. Save the human race in an ideal. Help them avoid our mistakes. And most importantly, KEEP GRUNGE ALIVE!!!

As he spoke these last words, a thump was heard off screen. Vincent immediately ran towards the sound. And then the alien heard a teenager's voice asking, "Is she alright?" followed by running footsteps. There was no answer for a brief period. Then Vic saw himself age thirteen turning off the camera with a tear running down his cheek. The image cut to black shortly after.

PART ONE: PEARL JAM

Vic Grunge started to cry remembering his parents and their death. Though he reminisced the last moments, his life before that was still a blur. His weepy depressive vision focused on the purple cover of one of the cassette cases. The band Pearl Jam in a circle holding their hands up high in the album called simply *TEN*. As his chest started to boil, the recording sent by his father started to make sense. The alien needed to contain the radioactivity in his upper body at all costs in order to help the Crystal People in Window World. Vic picked up the Walkman, opened the Pearl Jam case and introduced the cassette into the slot. He closed it and put the headphones over his ears.

PLAY

ONCE

Once upon a time, a psychotic alien wanted to control himself. The music didn't seem at all what he expected. It had a sadder feel to what was needed in that moment. But, somehow, it helped. It didn't make sense. Turns out the cure for sadness was sadness itself. Was it the start of his descent into madness? Destined to be a superhero, a killer... or something entirely different? The pressure in his chest started to calm down. The air was fresher and his hope for helping Window World increased with every passing moment. He recalled the map layout described by his father. Fortunately, the spaceship had a more elaborate chart with the names and cities which Vincent left out in his explanation.

From Ground Zero's perspective, the cities were located northeast, southeast, northwest and southwest. Their names were designated as zones in a specific color (blue, red, yellow and purple). They all were surrounded by high walls with a specific access point which, in every case, was close to him. He literally had to walk north, south, east and west and then make a right or left to enter each city. Though Ground Zero was extremely small and each entrance was only a song away. The alien continued to study the map in silence for the quest that lied ahead.

EVEN FLOW

Vic took the West Road and decided to start in the Purple Zone. Before stepping out, he saw an open closet by the door. Inside there were four flannel shirts like the ones his father had described. Interestingly enough, they were of the same colors of the cities. Inferring there was some cosmic significance behind it, he wore the purple flannel shirt thinking it was meant for the Purple City.

His spirits were high. But not as high as to make him blow up. Plain serenity. Sun in his face. Even. With a breeze of imaginary butterflies filling his spirit with calm. A homeless person without any worries. Not having a home really makes you a drifter. Somebody with a purpose. And a home is really something that lies within. Being at peace with your surroundings. Vic was somewhat worried about the Nuclear Bipolar issue. Would he be perceived as such? An insane alien homeless war hero you throw change at and never really respect?

At the end of the West Road, where the Purple City access was marked, the terrain became to take a turn for the worst. It was now mud. But not conventional mud. Sticky mud. Kind of like honey. A huge brown bee was waiting for him at the city gates.

STOP

The bee was on its legs, but appeared to be dead. Vic approached it with timid steps. He lifted his right hand slowly as if wanting to pet it. But then the bee reacted by suddenly fluttering its wings and hovering in front of him.

— DON'T TOUCH ME! — the bee screamed —. I'M SICK!

— My apologies — Vic said with remorse and fright —. I didn't mean to upset you.

— Nah, I'm kidding. You can touch me if you want. I am sick though.

— I'll take a rain check. Just wanted to check if you were fine.

— I'm not. But that's a good thing.

— Why?

— How else would you know how to find happiness?

— True...

— So, who the fuck are you?

— Excuse me?

— Kidding again. I know who you are. You're the Grunge Rock Alien.

— That's what they're calling me?

— Yep. You're lucky. It's a badass name. My name is just Bee.

— Yeah, it sucks. It's not creative at all. No offense.

— None taken. But, in my defense, that's what they call me.

— They?

— The Crystal People. I prefer to be called MUDRIDE.

— Let's stick with Bee.

— Now who's not being creative?

— Maybe if you didn't play in the mud all day, you could call yourself whatever you wanted.

— It doesn't matter if you come from the mud. What matters is the honey you create from it. Our actions are the only thing that must stick.

— Wow... that's very wise. Can I go through now?

— It's not that simple.

— How come?

— I was appointed the West Road Sentinel. You must answer my riddle to get through.

— A riddle? Really? I hate riddles! Since when did my Rock N' Roll quest become fucking Dungeons and Dragons?

— Don't blame me. I didn't make the rules. And don't you trash talk D&D ever again.

— I can't believe I'm saying this, but I rather be frisked by a giant bee.

— Trust me. You don't.

— Okay, let's have it.

— If I was divided by a rose, what's the color of the river I bathe in?

— That's totally incoherent.

— Think about it for a moment. In the meantime, I'll make some more mud honey!

— Are you gonna barf it, crap it or sculpt it? Wait... you know what? I don't want to know. Back to the riddle... it doesn't make any sense.

— That's why they call it a riddle, flannel boy.

— Okay... I can figure this out... let me think... you're brown... and roses are generally red. Brown is a mixture of green and red. So, I'm going to say green. A GREEN RIVER.

— Hey, not bad! It didn't take you that long. I thought you were going to be here for a while and it would start getting awkward when you realized you sucked at it.

— Sorry to disappoint.

— You may now pass, Grunge Rock Alien. Still... one last thing I must ask you...

— What's that?

— Are you sure you want to go in?

— Yes. Why?

— They're a bunch of assholes.

— Which ones?

— Um... all of them. Yeah, all of them.

— And you decided to tell me this after I solved your riddle?

— Just saying. You're better off in Ground Zero. But don't take my word for it. I'm a misanthropist insect who lives in the mud.

— I thought the term "misanthropy" applied only to humans.

— It does. I just didn't what you to feel left out.

— Thanks for that. But why keep working for them then?

— In your home planet nobody hates their boss? Sounds like Paradise! You have a lot of mud too, don't you?

— I think I'll take my chances with those assholes. See you around, Mudride.

— Wait!

— What?

— Always remember... LIFE DOESN'T GET EDDIE VEDDER!

— Yeah, that's cute.

PLAY

ALIVE

In spite of Bee's warning, Vic was optimistic and felt happy in the song's words. And even more alive once crossing the main gate towards the city. Inside, everything was purple. Purple city, purple people and purple skies enclosed like a dome. Though these people weren't actually people. Even if they looked like humans, they were made entirely out of glass.

The city was an exact replica of Seattle dipped in purple. But the strangest purpleness came from his own flannel shirt. It started to glow moments after crossing the gates. Before even realizing what was up, the alien was floating two feet above the ground. All because the purple flannel shirt had somehow given him superpowers!

Vic thrusted towards the skies displaying his ability to fly. With the song culminating in Mike McCrady's ethereal guitar solo, his joy grew by twirling in the air at high speeds. His flannel cape waving in the Wind. The alien felt that his powers didn't have to do with something within. In other words, the purple shirt controlled the airstream itself. In his overexcited frenzy, Vic tried going out of the planet but couldn't for some reason. Domed skies aside, the powers were limited to the color zone he was in.

This Icharus paradox made him think. For starters, Bipolar emotions started shifting in the opposite direction. His chest started to boil in his manic state. Aside from that, there was a possibility of scaring the locals with his capabilities and appearance. Maybe even the military would get involved and shoot him down. Something that was witnessed from the very start. Armies and armies of robots dressed like Nazis. But the sad part was that, not only did these bizarre robofascists didn't even mind he flew around unsupervised, but the citizens themselves didn't care that he was even there. Was being alive a curse?

WHY GO

While thinking about landing, Vic saw a very hot redhead plummeting to her death from the Smith Tower. She was human like him and was also in Grunge clothing. Specifically, a sleeveless Bikini Kill shirt with a flannel miniskirt. Vic flew down at incredible speed to save her and managed to catch her in his arms just as she was about to hit the pavement.

STOP

— Are you alright? — Vic asked placing her on the ground.

— Well, well, well — said the girl annoyed for surviving —. If it isn't the Grunge Rock Alien. Why couldn't you let me die?

— On Earth we say "thank you."

— But you're not on Earth, are you?

— I'm picking up a strange vibe here. Like nobody cares that I'm here and you hate me for some reason.

— You really don't know?

— Know what?

— I'll let you buy me a cup of coffee. Seeing how you saved a life not worth saving.

— Sorry I have a thing about preventing beauty from destroying itself.

— Fine, I'm buying. Your cheesy line worked on me for some reason.

— I couldn't have invited you anyways. I don't have any money.

— Here you pay with liquid. We have to give drops of blood. That's why it's called blood money or blood dollars.

— So, to function in this economy, I have to become fucking Emo. That's great.

— Become an Emo or die of starvation. Take your pick.

— Hunger strike.

— Save it for later. You'll understand why I fucking jumped. My name is Davanita, by the way.

— Call me Vic.

PLAY

Davanita smiled with such perfection that it sparked something inside of him. A feeling so great that it worried him because of his weird condition. But right then and there, he knew he didn't want to go to the home that no longer existed. Though the superhero couldn't help but think about his guide. Was she as mentally ill as him? Was this place her mental institution or was it the other way around?

The alien flew with his dream girl in his arms. Their destiny was the Starbucks in Pike Place Market. Since the Crystal People didn't need glasses for being glasses themselves, there were a series of hoses hanging from the ceiling that served as straws.

Davanita pinched her finger in one of the many slots surrounding the entrance. A ticket was printed out with five credits. She went to reserve a table and gave the ticket to Vic. As she walked away, Davanita pointed at the coffee machines. Vic understood the signal and approached the Douchey Hipster Purple Clerk at the counter.

STOP

— Good morning — Vic greeted—. Two coffees, please.

— Two coffees? — the Clerk said pompously—. You have to be a little bit more specific. We serve many varieties.

— Don't care. Just give me two coffees.

— Again, what type? Arabica, Robusta, Excelsa, Liberica? What about the blend? Roast date, Flavor Profile, Whole Bean, Roaster's Value? Coffee type? Latte, Expresso, Cappuccino, Mochaccino, Frappuccino? And would you be adding any spices? Pumpkin, cinnamon, ginger? With milk? Would it be whole milk, fat-free milk, soy milk, almond milk? Sugar? Would it be regular, brown, stevia, saccharin?

— Surprise me.

— You have to pick, sir.

— Okay... what if I told you I want two regular coffees.

— I would say you're in the wrong place.

— You sell coffee here, don't you?

— Of course!

— Then fill me up with leaded, bitch.

— Do you know how to read?

— Excuse me?

— Books. You should read and maybe you could learn how to talk and ask for things.

— And I suppose you read a lot of books and understand everything.

— I do. I read five books a week. I also watch independent films, listen to mainstream music and read manga comics from female authors.

— That doesn't make you smart. Especially if you only use the information to belittle the people around you.

— Are you calling me stupid??? I gain more knowledge in one day than you have in your entire lifespan!!!

— And yet... you work in a Coffee shop.

— It's a Starbucks! The first Starbucks of them all! Best coffee in Window World!

— It's a shame that the best coffee in the world has a douche like you to promote it. Still not impressed, by the way.

— I also work in a Book Store! I study, go to the gym and work two jobs. You have no idea how difficult that is!

— Oh, poor baby. That's called real life. There's nothing unique about it.

— You remind me of my father. He tells me all the time life will put me in my place. That I should appreciate him putting a roof over my head.

— Then he's a wise man.

— No, he's not! He's always wrong! I decided to never speak to him again! Not even a greeting for something terrible he said to my mom!

— Nobody is wrong all the time. Except people who actually believe that. And not talking to your dad ever again for something terrible he said? What are you? Six years old? The fact that you live with your parents and don't pay any bills makes you even more of a douche. You appear to be the type of person that somebody tells you "The sky is purple" and you say "Fuck no! It's blue."

— It is fucking blue!

— I rest my case.

— You don't know anything!

— I know enough. Crybaby, comes to mind.

— In that you are right, sir! You're going to make me cry!

— Though I would love to see that, please tell me what I can get for five credits?

— Five credits? That's two regular coffees.

— Oh, you got to be shitting me!!!

— What?

— Nothing— Vic said giving him the ticket and trying to contain himself—, just give me my coffees and I'll be on my way.

— Name?

— Vic.

— Rick?

— VIC.

— Okay, go to your table and the coffee will pump out once I call out your name. You must yell "PRESENT" for it to work.

— Great. Thanks for wasting my life.

— FYI, I'm going to register a complaint against you.

— Sorry?

— I'm offended. That's unacceptable.

— Shouldn't it be the other way around? Isn't the customer always right in this fucking planet?

— No, Mister Nick.

— IT'S VIC! AS IN VICTOR!

— Point being, you are not made of Crystal so you don't get a vote. NEXT!

Vic stepped aside and stared at him with hatred. His chest started to effervesce with nuclear characteristics as he walked towards Davanita. Fortunately, the very sight of her beauty calmed him down. The alien sat down and gazed at her for a moment. That face of an angel. Full lips and dark blue eyes. She was the "It" girl.

— DICK! — the Clerk screamed from the counter—. DICK!!! DIIIIIIIIICK!!!!!

— This is all just a sick joke — Vic said grumpily.

— Aren't you gonna answer, Dick? — Davanita asked trying to contain her laughter.

— Oh, you betcha— Vic answered comically while slightly turning his head towards the counter—. Present!

— DIIIIIIIICK! — the Clerk continued.

— PRESENT!!!!!

— Great — Davanita confirmed after hearing some whooshing sounds—. You can start drinking now. Careful, though. It's very hot.

— Duly noted— Vic said slurping carefully—. I'm surprised there wasn't a big line. Being the first Starbucks and all.

— Seattleites would never stand in the line. But the Market is different here than in your planet. There are no tourists. Even the Mexicans consider themselves Native.

— Mexicans?

— On the subject of waiting, what took you so long?

— The clerk was extremely douchey. It was very time consuming.

— Did he call you an asshole for insulting his douchey beliefs?

— No, he called me a dick. Many times, actually. Wait... you were there!

— Funny... this is nice... though it's not why I brought you here.

— Please don't end this by saying "YOU'RE ON CANDID CAMERA!" What do you know? I'm starting to remember trivial bullshit.

— It'll come back to you. Don't worry.

— Okay. So why don't you tell me something I don't know?

— When your father first contacted Window World, the Crystal People were very primitive. He promised to show them many technological perks if we welcomed you properly. At that time, everybody was incredibly excited about your arrival. That's why all the cities look like Seattle and clones like me were created.

— You're a clone?

— Yes. There are no real humans in Window World. Your father thought you might feel uneasy with the Crystal People's natural form, so he created one clone per city to guide you.

— You're my guide and you were going to kill yourself? Was it because of the torture of being my guide or because you wanted to lead me towards suicide?

Davanita laughed hard. Vic joined in shortly after. They stopped and stared at each other for a moment.

— JOKES ASIDE — VIC said in a serious voice—, why did you want to die?

— Honestly— Davanita answered—, I didn't even know that you were here. I gave up. You were my purpose and I couldn't wait any longer.

— You have to learn to be patient in life.

— Oh, I forgot to mention. This story I'm telling you, happened five hundred years ago.

— Five hundred years ago!!! How's that even possible???

— Clones don't grow older upon reaching a specific age. We are basically immortal unless killed. As for time, it goes by very slowly on Earth when compared to Window World. So, you can understand now why the new generations don't care about your arrival. You're a relic, yesterday's news, an oldie.

— The 90s aren't fucking oldies!

— Tell that to the Crystal People.

— What about my shirt?

— Your father designed chemically enhanced flannel shirts made to respond to our atmosphere's color spectrum. A chemical reaction that enables you to have an element-based superpower in each city.

— Which element is for flying?

— Wind, genius.

— Okay... ignoring your sarcasm. You mean I have more Wind-based powers?

— Yes. Depends on your creativity. Regardless of my sarcastic pun, note you can also acquire flight capabilities with other elements.

— What are the superpowers even for?

— I think your father knew the time issue was going to be a problem. He probably thought you would gain more popularity as a superhero than a simple man. That or he wanted you to save us. Help us in our time of need.

— I'll do my best. Heck, I already rescued one pretty lady today.

— That's sweet, Vic. Now it's your turn to teach me.

— Teach you what?

— Everything.

Vic and Davanita kissed right there. Romantically. Then fervently. Escalating to the climax of their mutual attraction. They finished their coffees and exited the Starbucks by the pig.

PLAY

PLAY

BLACK

Vic flew Davanita to her apartment. It was very close from the Market as it was pointed out by the beautiful clone. They continued to kiss and began to undress very quickly. The alien put his Walkman down for the very first time.

STOP

They made love soon after. Passionate love. Real love. She was an artist. And they made art that night. Surrounded by empty canvas paintings, clay sculptures and broken glass pictures. Vic summoned his flannel midway by synching to the airstream of the open windows. They started spinning and spinning with the shirt's powers and continued the lovemaking on the bedroom ceiling. A part of him felt afraid. He figured sex is the ultimate nuclear detonator. And love... let's just say that if it can create worlds, it can destroy them just as easily. And that was the problem. Vic was experiencing everything as if he was a new born. His manic libido was also altering his chest chemistry. Quickly experiencing the most dangerous emotion of all. There in her bed and full of expectations, his life was about to change.

— I think I'm falling for you — Vic said smiling with high hopes.

— Don't say that — Davanita alleged with a serious tone.

— Why not?

— Because... I'm engaged... to a Shot Glass... I'm sorry.

— A Shot Glass?

— Yes, he's the leader of the Vegan Tequila Cartel. They run this city. So, your life is also in danger.

— A SHOT GLASS???

— That's what you're worried about?

— I don't care about dying. I care that you're engaged to a fucking Shot Glass! Hold on... I'm confused. Is it a literal Shot Glass or is it some sort of Window World slang?

— A midget.

— Oh... not that I buy into this whole PC crap, but I think they're supposed to be called "little people."

— You mean Shot Glasses.

— WHATEVER!

— I think I should go.

— No... wait. There must be something I can do.

— My fiancé is very dangerous. Tony will kill you once he knows what happened between us. He has taken all the Purple Women hostage in the Aquarium by Pier 59. I agreed to marry him if he set them free.

— I can rescue them. I can rescue you!

— No woman needs to be saved— Davanita said arrogantly as she got dressed—. We can handle our own problems. And this is how I solve mine.

— Why would you try to kill yourself then? — Vic pointed out.

— I thought his proposal would lose its leverage and they would be set free. He only captured them because of me. But now I see I have to marry him. If you really want to help me, just leave me alone.

Davanita left quickly without looking back. Vic didn't go after her...

PLAY

What once filled him, now left him empty. All colors washed in black. Her love in the hands of another man... glass... whatever. He felt alone, rejected... dead. Love had cast a spell. An evil spell that wouldn't go away. The mere thought of her love... glowing in somebody else's heaven. Contemplating her light from the shadows. Realizing everything without her was meaningless. Even if it was against her will. An evil Cartel had taken hostage all those women. Was he supposed to listen to his love or rescue them all? There was no correct answer. But the problems of Window World were the least of his worries. His chest was now boiling to his demise. Like an atomic blender shredding his very Being. And he couldn't stop crying. Bipolar waterworks. Nothing like normal sadness. As if comparing a brook to a waterfall.

JEREMY

Vic dried his tears and decided to go out. Find some sort of distraction to reduce his radioactive depression. Flight and Grunge made him happy. But even while flying, the lyrics of the sixth track were somehow making him sadder. Inside grew a hunger for death. A need to die as soon as possible. To snuff it. Nothing mattered anymore. Everything was lost in a second. Suicide was his calling. It was in his nature. And in order to be alive, he had to live unnaturally. Go against his urges. His Death Wish. Something else was needed. Some meaning. Somebody to save. And then Vic came across a Crystal Boy in his early teens. Weeping without restrictions. As he wanted to weep in that moment... but couldn't. In the meantime, helping others would give him purpose.

STOP

— Why are you crying, kid? — Vic asked as he landed in front of him.

— You wouldn't get it— said the Crystal teen in a gloomy voice.

— Try me.

— Well... I want to kill myself.

— Why?

— I'm sick of it all. School, my parents...

— Let's go one step at a time. What's up in school? Are you being bullied?

— Yes. I'm not going anymore. I'm scared.

— You know how you can solve that?

— Shooting myself in front of everybody?

— WHAT? NO! Don't do that. That's horrible! Guns have no place in schools.

— Then why are there so many?

— Well, there shouldn't be. You're so much valuable. And you're not alone. You see this in my chest? I will explode if I get as sad as you.

21

— That is sad... you're depressed too?

— Half the time...

— You have any comforting words?

— Well... how's about... LIFE DOESN'T GET EDDIE VEDDER!

— Really? This is what you're telling me to lift my spirits?

— Sorry, kid. But it's true. If I have a divine shrink from the Heavens, his name is Eddie Vedder.

— Eddie who?

— I'll pretend I didn't hear that. Why don't you tell me about your parents?

— My mother left. My father hasn't been the same since. He doesn't pay any attention to me.

— I know for a fact that your mother has been kidnapped by what I understand to be a Mexican Vegan Drug Cartel. I will help you get her back and your father will be whole again. As for your bullies, I could go and scare them myself but it wouldn't change a thing. Sometimes you have to stand up for yourself. Maybe people won't like you, but at least they'll respect you.

— I'm just so... scared.

— I understand. I'm scared too, you know. It won't stop me from doing what I have to do.

— But aren't you the alien with superpowers?

— I am.

— I wouldn't be afraid if I had superpowers.

— Not having powers is the greatest power of all. You need to deal with the world without any shortcuts. And what makes a man is the long journey he needs to withstand. I do have powers but I can only use them for the greater good. And you're the greater good, buddy.

— Call me Jeremy. Though my real name is Jeremias. I'm Mexican, by the way.

— With respect to your family, Jeremy... why are there Mexicans here?

— We crossed the border.

— There are also people crossing the border on this planet?

— How else could we get here?

— I mean... from where did you cross the border?

— You can call it "crossing the border" but my mom calls it "searching for a dream."

— Never mind. But that's the point I wanted to make. You also need something to do. From my experience, depression grows from having no activity or purpose. If you wish to make your dreams come true, you must nurture each dream with hard work.

— What do you suggest?

— Depends on what you like.

— I love to watch movies.

— Try making them. You can even recreate the darkness you're telling me without hurting anybody. Since it's fiction, you can die, kill, destroy...

— Run crazy through the woods with the American flag as a cape?

— If that helps you.

— Filthy! And how do I make movies?

PLAY

Vic put on his headphones and smiled. The alien had already seen an electronic store while flying to meet him. He took Jeremy in his arms and flew him there incredibly fast. The alien bought him a digital camcorder with a pint of blood. Now Jeremy could record his movies. The depression associates said their farewells and somehow knew they would see each other again. Vic was still a bit shook up. Though Grunge was his medication, he still felt suicidal towards the end of the song. Couldn't be helped...

END SIDE 1. TAPE SWITCH. SIDE 2.

PLAY

OCEANS

Vic flew to the top of the Space Needle to reflect upon his dilemma. There was now an unspoken obligation to save Jeremy's mother. Which in turn would spare them both from killing themselves. Even though Davanita told him not to intervene, the alien had no choice as a superhero. Making the sacrifice of losing her for the greater good. Or... who knows? Maybe he could get the girl in the end...

Vic Grunge hovered upon the Puget Sound tucked in between land and oceans. Everything reminded him of her. The waves, the moonlight reflecting on the water, the romantic ferry rides, the breeze he could feel and manipulate... all spelled Davanita. It gave him faith. Though his objective was to help the Crystal People in general, he wanted to win her back most of all. Somehow make amends with his spirit. An embrace that would leave both souls intertwined in happiness. Vic wished with all his heart she was there. Bee's words came to mind. If not for misery and yearning, happiness would have no face. But he had to focus first. There was a Mexican Vegan Drug Cartel of "Shot Glasses" to fight.

The alien took to the skies until he reached Pier 59. The Cartel was already waiting for him in the Aquarium entrance where he landed. They were all little people and had many tattoos printed in their crystal skin such as "Tequila Sunrise of Death" and "Veganos Locos." Most were shirtless and wore baggie jeans. All of them were armed to the teeth. The leader and his main rival was the one in front wearing a Mexican hat with two six shooters. He had a long mustache like Yosemite Sam.

STOP

— Welcome to your end! — shouted the leader with a Chicano accent—. I'm Tony Tequila. I heard you slept with my woman. Now you're going to get it, homes! YOU'RE FUCKING DEAD!

— I got a better idea — Vic replied with a comical tone—. Why don't you break off the engagement and go fuck a lime slice?

— WHAT DID YOU SAY???

— While we're on the subject, there's something I need to get off my chest. I don't get the whole Vegan thing. Tequila comes from a plant. It's been bothering me since I first heard about you guys.

— Um... well there's also tequila made from animals, milk and eggs.

— No, there isn't. It's the blue agave plant. As I recently started to recall, it only grows in the Tequila region of Earth. Which also means your tequila is not technically tequila.

— I have no time for semantics, homes!

— But what are your customs? What do you consume? Why are you against eating meat when you only drink?

— You can also drink the blood of animals, ese. Much like our ancestors.

— If your ancestors drank the blood of animals, shouldn't you keep drinking it as well?

— Drinking animal blood is murder!

— And yet your ancestors drank it and you want to kill me. It boggles the mind.

— You like to drink blood, don't you?

— Do I look like a fucking vampire to you? I don't drink blood.... well maybe blood sausage, but that's it.

— I knew it! You consume meat. You sick fuck!

— I also love milkshakes with egg protein, asshole.

— Only the egg white?

— Of course. Wouldn't be a protein shake with the yolk.

— The yolk also has protein.

— As well as fat and cholesterol. It's not recommended for workouts.

— Soy has a lot of protein too.

— False. And don't tell me tofu tastes like meat.

— Tofu does taste like meat!

— By the way, do you know any good burger places around here? Real hamburgers. I mean non-vegan and non-liquid "drank from a hose" type hamburgers.

— Uneeda on Freemont. Best liquid burger you'll ever taste!

— Liquid burgers... fabulous.

— You can also grab a bag of Dick's.

— Go fuck yourself.

— The burgers.

— What?

— Dick's Drive In.

— Oh. My bad. You tried meat, milk and eggs, then?

— Si, papi. Many times. But I've changed my ways.

— To be vegan and kill people? Again, I'm very confused. I don't fucking care if you drink plant-based beverages. But at least try and make some goddamn sense.

— So now I'm stupid because I'm Mexican, Purple, Vegan and a Shot Glass???

— When did I say that? I'm saying you're stupid because your stupid. Being Mexican, Purple, Vegan or a Shot Glass has nothing to do with it. If you were eating fajitas only with peppers and onions, I'd be the happiest alien on the planet. But vegan tequila? C'MON!

— You're hurting our feelings, homes! We crack very easily!

— Well, that makes my job a whole lot easier. I can do it either way. Psychologically or physically. Though I'm kind of hoping for an actual fight. Because of the superpowers and all. Aside from winning back Davanita by beating the shit out of you.

— You'll get your wish then, *Alienigena*. KILL HIM!

PLAY

ALL THE SHOT GLASSES started shooting maize bullets from their ear of corn guns. Vic raised his hand and stopped all bullets in midair. He then reversed the momentum of the corn back to its origin and took out a lot of the Cartel members. The second infantry gang then proceeded to run towards him with eggplant machetes. Vic effortlessly created a small hurricane from the boarding waters to brush them aside and crack them into oblivion. The remaining Shot Glasses ran inside the Aquarium following Tony Tequila's orders.

What looked like a cowardly retreat, was really a clever counter tactic since Vic's Wind powers would be reduced in a closed environment. Aside from that, the Cartel freed the Giant Clams and rode them like horses. They were ten times larger than the ones on Earth and were very hard to reach. At least for someone without powers of any kind or a fondness for basketball. Promisingly, Vic had both and was already remembering many things. Including 90s sports. He could no longer fly but could still make super-jumps. Super-monster-dunks to be more precise. And with this in mind, the superhero cried out:

— Well, time to fuck you up Shawn Kemp Supersonic style!

Vic grabbed a live anemone and covered it in a wind bubble to make it bounce like a basketball. He proceeded to dribble and slam dunk over their heads. Cracking their crystal skulls one after the other. The tribute to the Reign Man was met by performing the one-handed throwdown, double pump reverse, roundhouse righthanded slam and, of course, the Lister Blister. Once free of the Clam Riders, Vic used Wind like telekinesis to push the remaining Cartel infantry out of the way and disabling their arsenal. Which required very little of his Wind potential. In the end, he was again face to face with Tony Tequila who lay half cracked and afraid on the ground.

STOP

— You're done, amigo— Vic said with a smirk.

— No, please! — cried Tony in horror—. Spare my life, homes! If you do, I will fill you in on a little secret.

— I don't need anything from you. I only want to free the Crystal Women and end you so Davanita and I can be together.

— *Ay, pobrecito*. You really are that gullible, aren't you?

— What do you mean?

— We're not a Cartel. We're not even vegan. I came up with the whole badass image with eco-friendly tendencies.

— Do you even know what "eco-friendly" means? Hint, it's not vegan tequila.

— Okay, okay! So, I fucked up with the vegan shit! But the rest is true.

— Are you saying somebody planned this?

— Not just somebody. Your lady love, ese. The one you call Davanita. She hired us.

— For the sake of argument, why would she do such a thing?

— She has issues, papi. I mean real dark-fucked up-shrink-committing-suicide issues.

— And why should I believe you?

— You don't have to. Soon she will reveal herself to you... very soon.

— So... you're an actor?

— Yes and you massacred my entire actor's studio! If it wasn't for the millions in blood dollars she paid us, we would have turned back.

— It's what you get for becoming mercenaries. Yet, it could have been worse. I could have sent them to Window World Hollywood.

— Will you spare me?

— Only if your story checks out. In other words, you're coming with me.

Vic freed the women and tied up the fake Vegan Drug Lord. He sent a Wind based telepathic message to Jeremy. The kid replied that they were to meet in the Market by the pig. Moments before leaving, he caught a glimpse of a group of human babies swimming in one of the aquariums. But realizing his own insanity, the alien decided to ignore this vision and kept moving.

PLAY

PORCH

Vic met quickly with Jeremy who also brought him a liquid burger from Dick's. Tony Tequila was left tied-up in his custody. The alien then flew to Bellevue in search of his girlfriend. Apparently, the artsy apartment where they made love wasn't even hers. Davanita's real home address was given to him by one of the women held hostage. It was a typical American home with a distinctive large porch in the entrance. Little did he know that by stepping on said porch, his mind started to race with manic thoughts that made his upper body boil:

Well, there's the door... Should I knock?... Barge in?... Declare my love?... Shove a note under the door saying "did you set me up?" ... I can't do this... C'mon, you pussy... Do it! ... What if it's true?... Ordinarily I wouldn't give a shit... But I'm feeling so much... Love... Maybe I'm afraid of fucking it all up... And, by accusing her, there's no turning back... The confrontation will kill any future relationship... Yet... Was there any real future with that woman to begin with?... She's a feisty one... Extremely negative... Like me... Two negatives only make a positive in math... We would fight... A lot... No fucking egg shells... More like walking over a minefield... Every day... Explosion after explosion... Driving each other insane until there was nothing... And yet, I wouldn't leave... If she hit me? ... I wouldn't leave... I would bear it... Is that how love is measured?... By putting up with someone?... Her pain is my pain... But for how long?... Is this the last time I see you?... The last time to hold your hand and kiss you? ... It could end any day... It could end today... The routine keeps us together... I help you with the mortgage and pay for fancy dinners... I lose money... a lot of money... Another loan... Another fight... No balance... No middle path... Is this the end?... Now you're pregnant... Abort... Prochoice... Who wants a supervillain's baby anyways? ... You're a woman with a right to choose... But as the pregnancy ends, do we end as well?... Buy a cat... Kitten... She doesn't want me to leave... I've been poisoned... Toxic love... My kitten won't stop scratching me... Maybe I'm the dog that needs to be put down... But I live... And I don't leave... I stick... But why?... Why don't you end it either?... We talk about ending it, but it never happens... Today might be the day... I won't see her again after this... Ever again... I know it... We're both too radical... Our souls are passed their expiration date... It's over... One fight... It's all it takes to bring down our house of cards... We both knew this day would come... Bye, Davanita... There's no other way... I'm sorry... I know now what I must do...

Vic left the porch.

GARDEN

The Grunge Rock Alien flew into the rain. His chest was bubbling hot. Favorably, the burger and his music calmed him down. Much time was needed to reflect. While normal folk would go to a social gathering or call a friend, Bipolars felt best surrounded by the death they craved. And that's were fate took him. The graveyard. Lake View Cemetery. Where everything was in its place. Labeled with meaning. Names and deeds summed up in a phrase. A garden of rocks aligned with purpose. But all for what? Was there an afterlife? He used to think so. At least as far as his memories could reach. But all his pain and suffering drowned him in nihilism. There was no faith left in him. No belief there was even a God. How could there be any hope in his life? His first love had deceived him. Or was it Tony who lied to save his own skin? Either way, the result was no love for humanity or the Crystal People. And if there was no love for the people, how could he be a hero?

While these thoughts lingered in his mind, Vic came across two celebrity gravestones. It was none other than Bruce and Brandon Lee. He remembered being both a fan of martial arts and dark 90s movies. The strange part was, both appeared to him as ghostly figures. Bruce was wearing his yellow suit from Game of Death and Brandon was in his mythical Crow costume.

STOP

— Welcome, Vic Grunge — said Bruce in a relaxed voiced while his son watched in silence.

— Wow! — Vic gasped with excitement—. You know who I am? I can't believe it! Wait... how can you be here if you were buried on Earth?

— Names are keys in the astral plane. One must simply write or say that word to unite one realm with another.

— Like your graves?

— Precisely. But we're also here to aid you in your time of need.

— Is it that obvious?

— Even to the dead.

— I'm really lost, Mister Lee. I don't know what to do. It sucks because, truthfully, LIFE DOESN'T GET EDDIE VEDDER!!!

— I hate being a ghost because I can't hit you for that remark.

— Eddie's surfboards don't hit back?

— You're making it worse.

— Sorry.

— Tell me your troubles.

— I don't believe in anything anymore. I have no faith whatsoever. Not only in God almighty. I mean in my regular tasks and people.

— People are how they are. Do not pray for an easy life, pray for the strength to endure a difficult one.

— That's the thing. Pray to what?

— Is not our apparition proof enough of an afterlife and a God.

— It could also be my insanity.

— You have to believe as everybody else, my son. We have more faith in what we imitate than in what we originate.

— Imitate the humans or the Crystal People? It's all very confusing. There are too many things to think about. I don't want to let everybody down.

— There are many perils in this world, Vic Grunge. Failure is inevitable when searching for success. That's why in great attempts, it is glorious even to fail.

— Your words are very wise, Mister Lee. Though I don't get the meaning behind them.

— Stop whining and buck up — Brandon summarized —. Is that clear enough for you?

— Right as Seattle Rain— Vic said bowing his head.

— There's your answer! — Bruce cried out—. As Seattle's foul weather, you must be there for them even if they don't like it.

— Please say it. I need to hear it.

— I'm sick of saying it.

— C'mon! For me?

— Okay... fine. BE WATER, MY FRIEND.

— Thanks! Time to fulfill my purpose in life.

— Remember purpose comes after one's actions. Not before them. You will also receive our assistance in battle. Never underestimate your enemy.

— Even with my Wind powers?

— It makes no difference. You can never invite the Wind, but you must leave the window open.

— Does that mean you're going with me?

— In a way — said Bruce appearing a pair of purple nunchucks with built in speakers and knobs—. Take this weapon. You will need it when the time comes.

— How loud are they? — said Vic grabbing the floating nunchucks while focusing on the speakers.

— The frequency can reach 20.000 hertz. A force in the universe equal only to the combined decibels of the Gossard and Ament Grunge aura aligned with the Krusen percussion accurateness. Use these Distortion Nunchucks wisely, my student. I will guide your hand with skill as I imagine you haven't used nunchucks before.

— That is correct, my master.

— You can also summon me — Brandon intervened—. My presence can only assist you once. So, be sure that you contact me for the right reasons.

— How do I call you? — Vic asked.

— By saying the magic words: "It can't rain all the time."

— What will you do exactly?

— Let's just say it will be extremely badass and fucking hardcore.

— Language — Bruce replied morally.

— Sorry, father — Brandon rectified.

PLAY

Bruce and Brandon disappeared shortly after. Vic's purpose grew strong as he smiled with wicked joy. His manic state was acting up again. Luckily, the music helped a lot. In the end, Grunge was his religion and there were many idols to cherish.

DEEP

Vic flew over the purple Seattle skyline when something caught his eye. It was a feminist protest with all the Crystal Women he had saved. They were destroying everything in their path with weapons of many sorts. The Nazi Robot army was protecting them in the back and on both flanks. No men dared cross their paths and were all in hiding. Not knowing if the radical feminists would kill them on sight. Sadly, Vic saw that his lady love was their leader. She was dressed in a purple spandex bodysuit and was shouting through a megaphone, "MEN ARE WORTHLESS! WE ONLY NEED THEIR SEED!"

Apparently, Tony was right about her. His deepest fears had come true and his former conviction to stop her filled his mind with doubt. But Brandon Lee said it best. He had to stop being a crybaby and do what had to be done. Vic landed fast in a sonic boom and classic superhero pose; taking a knee, eyes forward, his right hand on the ground and his left arm to the side. Davanita raised her fist to signal her army to stop. She smiled in a malicious way.

STOP

— What do you know? — she said confidently—. My ex-boyfriend decided to show.

— Ex-boyfriend? — Vic replied satirically —. Are you so evil you broke up with me without me even knowing about it? I mean, not even a messenger pigeon giving me the "it's not you, it's me" routine? That's cold.

— I only needed you to give these women perspective of how things really are.

— I don't think that's true. You're using them too, Davanita.

— Don't call me that. I used that name to draw you in. Same as the damsel in distress suicide attempt and the Bikini Kill T-shirt.

— I think both the PJ and BK blasphemy hurt more than the broken heart.

— That's the whole idea.

— So, what should I call you? Feminazi?

— I'm not a Nazi.

— Your robots are literally wearing uniforms with swastikas.

— Fine, I admit it. I dig Nazi fashion. Another clone helped me with the tech part, but I assembled the robots myself from an indestructible mineral we call Deaf Metal.

— Death Metal? — Vic asked showing the heavy metal horn sign.

— No — she said rolling her eyes—, DEAF Metal. We named it that because it makes absolutely no sound when you forge it.

— Wouldn't know. I'm more into Hard Rock.

— Anyways, I thought the uniforms looked awesome.

— Aside from purple being the color of feminism, don't you wish deep down that the Purple Women where white? And to top it off, not Mexican, Jewish, Gay or Crystal?

— Well... yeah.

— Then you're a Nazi, my dear. Though I actually meant it as a synonym for radical feminist.

— When you put it that way, you may call me Feminazi.

— Why are you doing this?

— Why? BECAUSE OF YOU! Do you recall clones can't die of natural causes? I've been waiting for you for five hundred years. I FUCKING HATE YOU! YOU MISOGYNOUS BASTARD!

— I'm not misogynous.

— Any proof of that?

— I love you. How's that?

— You really think it's love? Did I mention I have a superpower that can increase my pheromones exponentially to make you fall head over heels for me? It's a ruse. All of it was.

— The thing about illusions is they fade away. And pheromones would only work if I'm near you. Love is something that sticks and makes you sick. Especially if the person you love is no longer there.

— Why do you think I slept with you and did all that Grunge oriented bullshit? Pheromones need roots too. By performing these tasks, my attractiveness would cling to you no matter what. Sure enough, you don't fall in love with the woman herself, but with her archetype. The illusion you create of that person fueled by basic sexual desire. In which case love is no more than an obsession chemically manipulated to perfection.

— Stop all this nonsense. Men and women are meant to be equals. Women are better than men in many things as men are better in others. We're not the same, but neither gender is better or worse. Trying to put women over men is just as stupid as the macho assholes in my planet that oppressed women's rights in the past. Instead of fighting for superiority, we should work as a team for a better future. Starting with you and me... together.

— Don't fucking sweet talk me! I'm not a fucking housewife that you can sway with your sad little speech!

— A housewife's job is as difficult and enduring as any other job. The only sexist thing about it is for the husband not to support a woman's right to do anything else.

— What if there was no husband? What if the first dozen Purple Men in my life treated me like shit and left me by the side of the road? You have no idea how much I suffered on my own!

— Everybody gets fucked eventually. That doesn't make you special nor does it justify making others suffer. I'm sorry I wasn't there for you before. But I'm here for you now.

— Sorry, Grunge Rock Alien. You showed up extremely late for our date night. Now you must die at the hands of the women you saved!

— Leave the Crystal Women out of this. I'm sure they won't follow you if they know the truth.

— What truth?

— JEREMY! — Vic yelled to the kid who had his camcorder hooked up to a giant screen—. ACTION!

Jeremy's first movie experiment was now playing in a theater near you. The screen revealed Tony Tequila spilling his guts about Feminazi's entire conspiracy.

PLAY

The Crystal Women watched in silence and gasped when they realized they were duped as they already doubted Feminazi's intentions in her dialogue with the superhero. They started cursing and threatening their leader. To which Feminazi remained unemotional and commanded her robot army to attack all citizens. Men and women alike!

RELEASE

Furthermore, the supervillain had one more Ace in the hole just as Vic was thinking of tearing the robots apart with his Wind powers. She took out a spheric Deaf Metal speaker that fit in the palm of her hand. It was purple like everything else there. But it was really something more sinister. And she had no objection in telling him its function before using it.

STOP

— You know what this is? — Feminazi asked while showing him the spheric purple speaker.

— Some sort of feminist contraption that reminds me to get you flowers on Valentine's Day? — Vic said humorously knowing in his heart he already lost her.

— No, you idiot. It's a present from your father.

— My father?

— It's funny, but your dad didn't actually trust you. He made a nuclear deterrent for all the clones in case you lost your mind. As somebody with Bipolar Disorder, you might go mad with your powers and destroy us all. The clones were not only meant to guide you, but to stop you. My pheromones are also proof of that. Considering they only work on humans and you're the only man I was created to be in contact with.

— I don't believe that my father would do such a thing.

— Believe it, Pearl Jam boy. It's ironic how I'm going to beat you with it when you're fulfilling your goody-two-shoes bullshit.

— We'll see about that — Vic said summoning his superpowers.

— Doom Orb — Feminazi called to the dot speaker —. PLAY REGGAETON!

— FUCK... NOW I GOT SHIT.

Soon after, the sphere played the worst music to ever materialize into existence. And it wasn't just bad. It affected him physically. Made him sick and weak. But that wasn't the unfortunate part. He lost his Wind Powers entirely. Not only a percentage of them like when facing the Cartel in the Aquarium. They were all gone. His Walkman was also affected by it. There was no way to press Play and phase out that horrible noise. No escape. No release. From the betrayal... from his love... from his father.

Vic was now a regular human being. And no match for Feminazi and her army of robots who had begun breaking Crystal men and women alike. He had to save them somehow. And then the hero remembered the gift from Bruce Lee.

— KILL ZE AÜSLANDER! — one of the Nazi Robots shouted with its mechanical German accent—. SNELL!

— Guten Tag, supercomputer fuckers— Vic responded amusingly—. I think you're in dire need of some Tech Support.

The alien took out the Distortion Nunchucks and cranked up the volume in the adjusted knobs. It was unclear what sound they would emit. As he was unsure on using the nunchucks themselves (having no martial art training whatsoever). But surprisingly, the alien started employing them as well as his Master. It was filled with Bruce Lee's spirit after all. And Feminazi couldn't believe her eyes. Especially when the sound was revealed as Lee's signature scream. A shriek so powerful that it could break the robots like paper. It turns out the only weakness for Deaf Metal was deafness itself by means of a high frequency sound. And nothing was higher that the frequency of a Bruce Lee war cry.

Vic manipulated the nunchucks left to right, over his shoulders, to his back while cracking every robot with a high-pitched distortion wave. Even in his weakened state, he swam across them with great skill. Tearing them limb from limb while leaving a trail of scraps in his tracks. He eluded punches and kicks while, at the same time, focusing on the Crystal men, women and children that were in danger. In that moment, Vic really felt like a superhero. Before, all his problems were solely fixated on him. When meaning comes from helping others. Purpose is really a function for the collective. Not for one individually.

The Grunge Rock Alien vanquished the entire robot army but noticed Feminazi's Doom Orb also provided her with an impenetrable force field. One that was not affected by the Distortion Nunchucks. Only something invisible could pass through. While pondering on the solution, Feminazi walked closer to him. The reggaeton music was affecting him even worse. No longer being able to stand and brought to his knees by a force of unspeakable pain. Such was the frequency, that the Distortion Nunchucks exploded like glass. A few inches from him, Vic was laying down on his back waiting for the final deathblow which Feminazi would deliver in the form of a Deaf Metal katana she recently drew.

— Heart over Reason— Feminazi said while placing the tip of her katana on his left pectoral —. A broken love enough to make you lose your mind. And now, I end you as the heartless and mindless man that you are. Any last words? You're about to become a ghost.

— Ghost— Vic said realizing something in his frail state—. That's it!

— Those are your last words???

— Nope.

— Please don't say "I love you." Have some dignity, for fuck's sake.

— It can't rain all the time.

— Really? What are you a pussy? It's just a little mist. That's the final message you want to be remembered by?

— Not exactly.

As he spoke these final words, a spectral crow appeared out of nowhere. It crossed the force field and nabbed the Doom Orb in its beak. The crow then threw the purple sphere into Brandon Lee's hand who immediately hurled it towards the sky. The dark vigilante then shot the Doom Orb repeatedly with a Mossberg 500 Cruiser without letting it touch the ground. Half way through the beautiful disaster, the reggaeton music stopped which in turn made Feminazi's force field disappear. Vic started to float in a purple aura with Wind flowing around him and indigo light flashing from his eyes. Feminazi was staggered. The alien only smiled at her.

PLAY

In spite of having the advantage, Vic contained himself. Pulled his punches. No longer knowing if it was out of devotion or her pheromone frenzy. Maybe that's what love was. Taking in too much of a good thing until becoming addicted. With the worst withdrawal of any drug. Aside from that, he felt incapable of hitting a woman. So, he forged a Wind Sword for himself out of thin air and started dueling with her. There was no need to hold the sword in his hand. It could be controlled by telekinesis. Feminazi had a lot of skills with the katana and it wasn't easy to bring her down. The fight when on for a while but she eventually realized the alien was holding back. She taunted him to take it up a notch. To which Vic only used the Wind to push her back or levitate and drop her from a safe altitude. Subsequently, taking her katana away. Feminazi sneered with confidence.

STOP

— You won't finish me off, will you? — the supervillain said with pride —. My pheromones are at full capacity. Or is it love... that you're feeling?

— Thanks— Vic responded—. Now I'll have that fucking song in my head all day!

— Nevertheless, your feelings for me are your weakness. It's how women can reign supreme. After my first bad experiences with men, I figured out I could destroy any man just by being hot and faking interest. Even without pheromones, it's all about saying you're not having any sex at all and then never giving them any in the long run. By getting them to believe the first part, you got them on the hook. And the obsession begins...

— Wow. That would make a great perfume commercial.

— Oh, I'm so much more than that. You're wrong about men and women. We're the superior gender. Smarter and much more capable than any male in the universe. We're the bringers of life and order while men only bring chaos and death. In the end, I'm going to herd in men for their seed like Asa Mercer herded his girls to the northwest as if they were cattle.

— Be honest... this is all because I left the toilet seat up, isn't it?

— Your fucking jokes won't be so funny once women inherit the planet.

— You forget no Crystal Women are buying into your supremacy crap.

— Then I'll clone myself. I think it's the best solution. They'll be white too. And there will be no need for men and their seed after all. Nor the Crystal Women that betrayed me. THEY WILL ALL DIE!!!

— You do know Hitler wasn't too fond of redheads?

— Couldn't care less what a man thinks. Including him. Women are the real Aryan gender. My city will be a female Nation of clones designed for superiority. Besides, my red hair is not a recessive trait. I was originally blonde and it changed color due to natural pheromone usage. Though it only works on humans, I can only control part of it.

— You're not a natural redhead? I am shocked... SHOCKED TO SAY THE LEAST, FRAULEIN! But you're wrong about something else too. Despite the pheromones and the genocide threats, I believe in my heart that I love you. It doesn't mean I won't do what has to be done.

— You need balls for that, honey. Something you were born without. That's why you're going to lose!!! Do you hear me? YOU'RE GOING TO...

Half way through her sentence, Vic created a bubble around her head which deprived her of air. She fainted shortly after.

— Did you... kill her? — Jeremy asked walking closer with all the Crystal People behind him.

— No— Vic answered—. She's just unconscious.

— Because you love her? Or was it the balls thing?

— Can't have balls without love, kid.

— But what will you do with her? There are no prisons in the Purple Zone.

— Really? Why?

— We were meant to be a utopia where there was no crime after your arrival.

— Don't worry. I'll think of something.

— Will you be the new candidate to rule us?

— Not likely.

— Who then?

— How about you?

— It doesn't work that way.

— Don't you have presidential elections?

— No — Jeremy alleged pointing at a muddy homeless Crystal man loitering in front of a bus—, we use to elect who ever could wash Master Slave Dirty Frank. The Vegan Tequila Cartel was the last group to accomplish that. Even if they were pawns in your ex-girlfriend's puppet regime.

— Hey — Dirty Frank said with a heavy metal horn salute.

— How's it going? — Vic saluted confused—. I think it's easier with democracy.

— How? — Jeremy asked.

— ANYBODY IN FAVOR OF THE KID RULING THE PURPLE ZONE SAY "AYE!"

— AYE! — everybody responded.

— See? — Vic acknowledged —. That easy. Long live King Jeremy.

— The wicked! — the kid added.

— No! You play nice!

— Okay, okay. I was kidding. Thanks, by the way... for saving me... from myself.

— Always wanted to save you, Jeremy.

— Then you really are our hero... out of curiosity, what would have been your last words?

Vic saw that the Crow continued to shoot the Doom Orb without letting it touch the ground and what appeared to be unlimited ammo. Seeing this, the alien answered the boy:

— LIFE DOESN'T GET EDDIE VEDDER!

PLAY

VIC REALIZED HIS FLANNEL shirt had another special power. One that came at a price. Since there were no prisons, he needed to build one in order to contain somebody as dangerous as his Ex. Yet the answer was with him all along. It was hard to explain, but sometimes he felt the shirt spoke to him on an intuitive level. And in this case, it said the supervillain needed to be tied down with the flannel itself. Feminazi had the shirt wrapped around her waist which in turn restrained her wrists and toes in Wind cuffs. Vic lost his Wind powers but knew it didn't matter anymore now that the Purple Zone was secure.

TAPE STOPPED

A while later, the Alternative Valkyrie appeared before him as a hologram. It turned out the deity was only a marble statue of a woman dressed in armor riding a winged horse. Not a physical person like he expected. The strange part being the statue had his mother's face. Even with all these bizarre details, Vic Grunge got down on one knee and expressed his sorrow:

— Bless me Goddess, for I have sinned. I wanted to hang myself with the coffee hoses. Beat the shit out of the Clerk and then send a picture to his father saying "Fucker's been put in his place." Had a hankering for vegan tequila eggnog with cobra blood. Though I enjoyed making love to Davanita, I wanted to fuck her without scruples once I knew she was a Nazi and a villain. I mean manic fueled no holds barred sexual intercourse of the filthiest kind and her Aryan clones popping in midway with some lesbic action in a kingdom where I am the only man. By the way, apologies in advance for jerking off to this image in the future.

Vic got up and was surprised by a piece of paper falling from the sky. The only word appearing therein was "HOPE." The divine apparition then proceeded to teleport him back to Ground Zero in an unconscious state.

PART TWO:
SOUNDGARDEN

As Vic woke from a long power nap, his memory was intact and he remembered all his heroic deeds in the Purple Zone. But his eyes quickly fixated on one of the cassette covers with an orange blob over an upside-down burning forest labeled *SUPERUNKNOWN* by the band Soundgarden. The alien replaced the Pearl Jam tape with the Soundgarden tape, put on the blue flannel shirt hanging in the closet and set course for the Zone of the same color.

PLAY

LET ME DROWN

Vic Grunge marched north through a forest where the Blue Zone was accessible according to the crossroad signs. Even lined up with personal purpose by helping the Crystal People, there were many expectations on his part for a measly recognition. They weren't that grateful. And that bothered him. A simple "thank you" would have sufficed. But nothing. No manners. No virtue. They went about their lives as if nothing had changed. Maybe just the kid. But Jeremy was their ruler now. Then there's the ex-girlfriend and father part. Vic felt betrayed by love itself. His father didn't trust him and his first love would have killed him without hesitation. He wanted to die. His chest was already bubbling with nuclear suicide. But the music helped... it always helped.

His dreams of death continued regardless. He wanted to go to Earth and die in his place of origin. Back in his mother's womb. Alone. With nobody bothering him. Drowned in a pleasure substance of some sort. In a haze of delight only the gods could whisper. But his death wish was interrupted by his duties. There was a mission to accomplish. Even though it still wasn't very clear what it was.

MY WAVE

Vic came across a river with a strong current. And there on the stream, something caught his eye. A crystal salamander grazing on a rock. There were small waves starting to push her off but she held her ground and remained there. This simple fact made him realize life is not only sacrifice. He had to help others but his own life and goals were equally important. The salamander was tough, not because she fought against the waves, but because the waves were hers. She had domesticated nature at will. And once you find out who you are and what you're capable of, it doesn't matter what everybody else thinks. That was the secret of Fortitude.

The superhero crossed the river jumping over stones with great ease and continued the path up north. The journey was longer than the West Road. More extended than one song. Even if it was the same distance on the map, it took him two listens to get there. It was as if somebody was losing him on purpose. As if the woods themselves were changing. But soon he reached the gate. Though there was no Sentinel to meet him. Vic tried opening the door to the city but it was locked. He started to search all around and saw nobody. Not until his eyes took to the trees and an anomaly stood out in one of them. It appeared to be some sort of animal using camouflage to hide itself in the bark. Before he could make out the image, the strange figure made a leap and landed right in front of him.

STOP

— BUYAKASHA! — screamed a stout sprite composed entirely out of wood.

— JESUS CHRIST POSE! — Vic said in shock—. You almost gave me a fucking heart attack!

— Sorry. I get very bored around here.

— It's okay. Are you the Sentinel?

— Before I answer that, do I owe you money?

— No.

— Have I given you a disease of some sort?

— Nope.

— Do you feel like choking me?

— Of course not!

— Then yes, I am the North Road Sentinel.

— Please tell me what you asked me before was the riddle.

— Oh, I see! You're the Grunge Rock Alien everybody's talking about! You can call me Wood Goblin.

— I see Sentinels are named based on their physical appearance entirely.

— It's still better than Bee. If I had my way, I would be called TAD.

— Why Tad?

— Totally Awesome Dude!

— Sure, you are. Why don't you tell them?

— Fuck no. The Crystal People wouldn't go for that.

— Oh right. Forgot about the noncreative flock of glass.

— Tell me about it. Their sodas are incredibly expensive.

— Who cares about soda?

— I don't know. You brought it up.

— No, I didn't.

— Why did you call me Jack, then?

— I never called you Jack! Wait... you mean like lumberjack? Is that what you fear?

— No, I fear soda.

— Why?

— I have my reasons... how can we be truly hydrated if water itself is not real?

— You're just saying that because you're a tree.

— And does a tree not give you air? Would you like for that air to be filled with bubbles?

— I'm sorry. Is this the riddle?

— No, I'm just fucking with you. You know, because...

— You're bored. I get it. Can you tell me the riddle so I can be on my way?

— All right. Here goes: If you lick an Eight Way Santa, how many balls does God have?

— That's no riddle! It's a pornographic blasphemy of some sort!

— It is what it is. Answer or be gone, lumberman.

— Okay, okay. I don't think God even has balls. He wouldn't have reproductive organs for starters. But "licking Santa" must be slang for a psycho reactive substance. In which case, even if God had balls, they would be a hallucination. Hence, fake. So, the answer to all possible scenarios is the same: NONE.

— Correct! — the Sentinel confirmed opening the city gates—. Amazing mind fuck to get there, but you're right. You may pass!

— Thanks, Wood Goblin.

— My pleasure. Stay off the soda.

— Is soda a metaphor for assholes?

— Oh no. They're all assholes.

— Yeah, Bee warned me in the Purple City. I think they're fine now, though.

— Give them time... assholes always revert to their natural state. Unlike soda which fucks you over in the exact same way.

— I think I'm missing something... but I'll take your word on that. Take care of yourself, Tad.

— Good luck, my dear boy.

PLAY

FELL ON BLACK DAYS

Vic entered the Blue Zone but it wasn't completely blue as expected. Though the city was definitely a bluish version of Seattle, it was more futuristic. High tech. Aside from that, the Crystal people were two shades of blue and the sky was black as night. Lights turned on at temperature color. This had a negative impact on him psychologically. The alien thought everything was fine. He even felt glad that he helped the Purple People and made a difference. But Wood Goblin got him thinking. Does helping somebody matter if that somebody forgets you helped them out at all? Is the blue sky an illusion about the inevitable black? We believe we will always exist. Living out our happy lives thinking they will be the happiest. But, in reality, everything's black. We find sadness and then die. Depression was bursting from his chest. Grunge music aided him. But also, his new superpowers.

Before even considering what they would be, a bolt of lightning struck him amidst the dark sky he was cursing. This fully charged him and gave him Lightning powers. Vic started testing them on street junk that immediately turned to dust upon contact. All electronic objects could be controlled by him such as cars, street lamps and home appliances. His hands were also electromagnetic, so the metal around him could be manipulated telekinetically. But maybe the coolest part was jumping into the air. Vic couldn't fly like in the Purple Zone, but he could summon bolts of lightning from the atmosphere and swing on them like vines throughout the city. The superhero twirled, summersaulted and thrusted through the skies with a few seconds of immediate thunder after each bolt. Suddenly the black sky didn't seem so black. He owned it. Being able to harness light from his darkness. And that's what life really was. Turning those black days into pure light.

MAILMAN

Nonetheless, one other fact of life is that everything that rises, eventually falls. Especially when distracted by a nearby swarm of giant Cicadas dressed as police officers. That, added to his inexperience landing at high speeds, led to a great tumble. This wasn't falling in the street or a pile of garbage which would've actually been a good thing. Instead taking out three mailboxes that were bolted down to the sidewalk. Because of his superpowers, Vic was okay from the crash, but a disgruntled Crystal Postal Worker came marching towards him. His body was wrapped in a box that said "Fragile" with his head, arms and legs popping out.

STOP

— Goddamn you! — screamed the Light Blue Mailman—. You fucked it up!

— Fucked what up? — Vic said getting up and dusting his clothes.

— HELLOOOO? The fucking mailboxes!

— Oh... sorry.

— My piece of shit boss is going to fuck me over. Not only does he exploit me, but the son of a bitch stole my girlfriend. A girl who never gave me the time of day before. Whom I pursued time and time again. Once I wore her down and her sweet honey dew lips touched mine, this motherfucker came along and stole her from me without breaking a sweat. I'm so sad... I know I'm going down now.

— Why not take them with you?

— What?

— Vengeance. If you're gonna go down, why not take those assholes with you?

— Yes... revenge... REVENGE!!!!

— Calm down. It must be well thought out. An impulsive response has no art to it.

— Can there be art in violence?

— Only when you paint with blood.

— Yeah! Steal their money too!

— That came out wrong. I mean you don't need to actually hurt or steal from them. There could be a long-term psychological Hell you can create.

— Sending pizzas to their house every night?

— Something more elaborate, I'd say. Just in case your boss is an undercover Ninja Turtle.

— That sounds complicated. Will you help me?

— Um... yeah... why not?

PLAY

Vic and the Mailman had formed a vindictive alliance. Though Vic wanted to help in more superhero ways, he was in his debt for the mailbox incident. So, joining his vendetta was the only way to repay him. The matter of how they were going to get back at his boss and his ex-girlfriend was still a mystery to him. It had to be measured just right. Not too tough as to shatter the targets' fragile existence nor too soft that the Mailman would find it unsatisfying. Vic couldn't help but smile thinking how even vengeance had some sort of moral code.

They stalked the boss and ex-girlfriend thinking of ways to get them back. But nothing sprung to mind in that short time. As the Mailman got frustrated with every passing second, Vic started to feel uneasy knowing perfectly well that they needed to find a solution quick. Otherwise, the Mailman would do something drastic. His personality seemed a little off to him. And this coming from a Bipolar teenager with a nuclear bomb in his chest. At the same time, the alien wanted to help him in such a way he would not be implicated directly. Knowing how touchy that world was, anything would turn him from superhero to supervillain in an instant. And that's when he thought of a simple solution that displayed all these qualities.

STOP

Vic advised him to use psychological violence knowing well the Crystal People would get hurt just as much as a physical beating. Appealing to his work station, the alien suggested it could come in the form of a singing telegram.

Though he felt stupid about the whole plan, the Mailman took a liking to the idea. He told Vic to meet him by the pig in a while since the song had to be composed. And a few moments later, they met up and went to Kerry Park where their targets sat on a bench.

PLAY

Vic spied from a distance where he could lip-read the words uttered by the Postal Avenger and his targets. Both the boss and his ex-girlfriend where in shock when they saw the Mailman. Vic couldn't really tell at that point, but a sudden explosion answered his inquiries. The only words he could lip-read off the Mailman were, "If I'm sinking, then I'm taking you with me!" It wasn't really a singing telegram, but it made sense.

SUPERUNKNOWN

As his ill advice started to increase in remorse, the bizarre Cicadas from earlier surrounded him at gunpoint. Strange that in that scenario, the alien was the criminal and the insects were the cops.

STOP

— HUMMINA, HUMMINA! — said the Special Agent Cicada in charge.

Vic understood the implication even if the weird language was unknown to him. Though the alien could have easily escaped with his powers, he decided to play it by the book on this one. He raised his hands and got on his knees as a Cicada Cop came to cuff him shortly after. Two of them grabbed Vic by his shoulders and flew him to the police station. There, his flannel shirt was taken along with his Walkman and headphones. He was put in a cell. But not just any cell. A puffy pink cloud cell. Maybe made to adjust to the Crystal People's sensitive nature. Reason why it was also completely soundproof. And Vic, the Grunge Rock music lover that he was, could not enjoy the silence. Sorry, Depeche Mode.

Shortly after, he was moved to an interrogation room with a double glass mirror and a table with three chairs. One Cicada sat in the far end with a Light Blue Crystal Translator in the other. There was one more Cicada on his feet who appeared to be very irritated with him. They asked the alien to sit in the middle chair.

— HUMMINA, HUMMINA??? — said the last Cicada smashing his front legs on the table with fury —. Hummina, hummina, Hummina, hummina, HUMMINA? ... hummina, HUMMINA???

— What the fuck? — Vic said startled while sitting down.

— The officer wants to know if you're a terrorist— the Translator interpreted.

— CRRRRR — hummed the Cicada beside him while stroking his hair.

— He said that with that many "Humminas"? — Vic asked while looking at the one touching him.

— He's the Bad Cop — the Translator clarified —. Just go with it.

— The one caressing me is supposed to be the Good Cop? He's scaring the shit out of me.

— HUMMINA! — said the Good Cop Cicada smashing his legs on the table the same way.

— Great — added the alien—. Now I have two Bad Cops.

— You hurt his feelings — said the Translator.

— You know— Vic pointed out—, I get called a "pussy" a lot around here. But I think the real pussies here are everybody in Window World. Everything shatters you. Oh, you poor things! You want a tissue?

— HUMMINA, HUMMINA! — both Cicadas screamed while smashing their legs on the table at the same time.

— STOP DOING THAT! — Vic yelled very irritated—. Look, either charge me with something or let me walk.

— Hummina, hummina! — said the original Bad Cop Cicada throwing his Walkman and headphones in front of him—. Hummina, hummina...hummina... HUMMINA, HUMMINA!

— He says you broke the law—the Translator interpreted.

— I had nothing to do with the terrorist bombing— Vic said with assurance.

— Not the bombing. The noise.

— Noise?

— Yes, the Hush Cicada Corps oversee and enforce the Noise Law Act of 98. No loud noises are allowed. Which includes bombs and, in your case, music.

— Music is forbidden here???? Under whose authority?

— Black Silence. He's our ruler and the clone assigned to this area.

— At least this time the clone revealed himself as a bad guy from the start. In that case, I won't say anything more without a lawyer present.

— HUMMINA, HUMMINA! — said the former Good Cop with a serious face that looked exactly the same as his normal and nice face.

— Hummina, hummina, hummina — said a third Cicada that rushed in wearing a suit and carrying a briefcase—. Hummina, hummina, hummina... hummina... hummina, hummina, hummina.

— Who the fuck is this? — Vic asked confused.

— That's your lawyer— the Translator answered.

— I don't want a fucking Cicada lawyer! What about a Blue Lawyer?

— Those are private and cost more blood money. Cicada lawyers are civil servants appointed to you.

— Whatever. What did he say?

— Never admit that you love Grunge Music or that Chris Cornell is Jesus.

— BUT I DO LOVE GRUNGE MUSIC AND I DO THINK CHRIS CORNELL IS JESUS!!!

— HUMMINA, HUMMINA! — both Cicadas Cops shouted while pointing at him enthusiastically as if accusing him.

— There's one thing I don't get— the alien inquired.

— What's that? — asked the Translator.

— I don't see you translating back and they obviously can understand me. Why not speak English directly?

— They are speaking English. Though they can only articulate the word "HUMMINA." That's how Hummenese came to be.

— Well, I got a question for all of you brainiacs. If I was wearing headphones, how could I break the Noise Law?

— Hummina, hummina, hummina, hummina — the three Cicadas whispered amongst themselves followed by the first Bad Cop Cicada pointing at him—. HUMMINA, HUMMINA... Hummina!

— He says you're free to go regarding the Noise charges— the Translator alleged—, but you have to spend time in the Hole for calling them pussies. And some counseling afterwards for the Grunge blasphemies.

— Fine— Vic said rolling his eyes —. Can I at least keep my music?

— Hummina, hummina, hummina, hummina, hummina, hummina, HUMMINA, hummina — said the former Good Cop Cicada.

— Yes — the Blue one translated.

Vic shook his head in disbelief. He was taken to the Hole while Black Silence laughed having watched the whole scene on the other side of the mirror. The Hole was a puffier cloud cell. It wasn't soundproof and was filled with

Japanese kitty figurines saying "Banzai!" every five seconds in disarray. Thankfully, Vic could finally tune it out by listening to Grunge...

PLAY

The superhero lied down in his cloud bed. Thinking. Trying to piece together his purpose. One that was more and more absurd with every passing moment. Reflection was a big part of doing time. Minutes were like days and being left there would eventually drive him mad. What was he doing? What was this World? This Anti-World? Nothing made sense. Black skies, large Cicada Cops, Lightning Powers coming from his shirt, Mailman suicide bombers... it was crazy to even think about. This last part also filled him with regret. Feeling responsible for the bomb and the casualties. He started to sense this great fear for the first time in his life. Like every road taken was the wrong one. Everything was down when what he really wanted was the upside to it all.

His thoughts were mostly on the infamous supervillain known as Black Silence. What kind of a person would ban music considering it noise? He couldn't even picture it. A world without music. Without Grunge music. The worst Hell is the one without a soundtrack of Hell itself. It was eerie. Inconceivable. The Superunknown.

HEAD DOWN

A few minutes after, he was transferred to another room by two Hush Cicadas. Vic only wanted to keep listening to his music, but there was no time for peace of mind. Like everything in the life of a hero. They took him to see another Cicada wearing a lab coat. Most likely the counseling the other Cops had mentioned. Vic sat down and was left alone with the therapist.

STOP

— Hummina, Hummina, hummina — said the Cicada Shrink.

— Can we get a translator in here? — Vic said a bit uneasy.

— Hummina, Hummina, hummina — answered the shrink mimicking breathing in and out while redundantly using his legs to explain it.

— Oh, I get it. It's a breathing exercise.

Vic took deep breaths and exhaled while the Bug Therapist continued to mimic the exercise as before.

— Hummina... Hummina, hummina — said the Bug Psychiatrist pointing at a poster of a blue baby smiling.

— You want me to smile now? — Vic asked looking at the poster —. Why?

The Cicada took out an Equestrian whip from his coat and struck him hard on the leg.

— MOTHERFUCKER! — Vic cried irritated—. WHY THE FUCK DID YOU DO THAT??!!

— HUMMINA! — the Cicada Counsellor insisted tapping on the smiling baby poster.

— ALL RIGHT! I'LL FUCKING SMILE FOR YOU!

Vic put on a fake smile from cheek to cheek hoping the Cicada would leave him alone. But it turns out the Shrink was going to continue whipping him despite his false happiness. So, the alien decided to just sit there and take it. Even when tears ran down his face and his chest started to boil.

PLAY

Vic joyfully lost himself in Ben Shepherd's celestial mind-altering song. As the giant bug kept lashing at his legs, he thought about what the therapy was even for. That we must always smile in the face of tragedy? Though the meaning behind it was clear, it was also a means for the System to manipulate us into submission. Never showing the ugly side of life. And just like the baby in the poster, this was the way they programmed us since birth. Who was behind this System? Was it the notorious Black Silence or was there more? Pondering over this question, the alien could only smile.

BLACK HOLE SUN

Vic was released seconds later. His legs felt sore from the whipping. Even his face muscles were numb because of all the phony smiling. They gave him back his enchanted flannel shirt and he became a Lightning Bearer once again. The alien started swinging from bolt to bolt when something new showed up in the sky. A black hole of some sort that only appeared to swirl in the zenith sucking in the perpetual Seattle rain. It seemed to breathe in and out. As if it was washing it away. He couldn't get a good enough read to know its purpose since the lightning bolts could only take him up so far. A purple flannel shirt would come in handy right about now. But maybe there was another way.

Vic landed in the Alaskan Way by the Puget Sound and looked at the Blue People around him. They all had similar fake expressions as the ones experienced in the therapy room. Cell phones were their focus. As if they were being brainwashed. Was the Black Hole Sun responsible?

The superhero started bolt slinging across the skyline when a giant hologram appeared out of nowhere. He landed on the Seattle Tower and watched the message.

STOP

It was the television clown J.P. Patches saying his mythical daily check list with the words appearing below:

- Mind Mommy and *D*addy
- Wash han**D**s, face, neck, and ears
- C**O**mb hair
- Brush Te**E**th
- **D**rink your milk
- Eat al**L** of your food

- Say your **P**rayers
- **S**hare your toys
- Put toys **A**way
- Hang up clothes**.**

The hologram disappeared moments later. Even if it was meant for kids, there was definitely some sort of hidden message. The black bold letters were curious. As if it was written in code to be decrypted. While reflecting on this, he saw a Light Blue Person being mugged by a Dark Blue Person. He swung down with ease now that he had mastered landings. Both were startled upon his arrival.

— FREEZE, PECKERWOOD! — screamed the mugger pointing the gun at the superhero.

— Hmm, tempting — said Vic with indifference while taking his gun away with electromagnetism —. But it's much more fun to kick the shit out of you while practicing my Zumba.

— We ain't done, a'ight! You gonna be darker than my skin, dawg! Grim Reaper will take you out and show you the blackest side of death! Out of the blue and into the black!

— NEIL YOUNG!

— What?

— I remember Neil Young! KEEP ON ROCKIN' IN THE FREE WORLD, YOU SON OF A BITCH!!!

— Tha' fuck?

— On that note, why are there light and dark skins here?

— So, you coming right at the brother. You racist sack of shit!

— Me racist? Didn't you call me a peckerwood before?

— I'm allowed to dis you. 'Cause of my history, it's my right to call you a fucking peckerwood.

— Mugger history?

— Oh, now you think all brothers are muggers?

— No, I think all races of muggers are pieces of shit. Light ones too.

— You're saying I'm better than him because my skin is lighter? — the Light Blue victim finally stated offended by the comment.

— Here we go — Vic said scoffing shortly after.

— I'm not better than him because I'm lighter! You racist fuck!

— Helloooo? He just mugged you and I saved you!

— I don't want to be saved by a bigot!

— Peckerwood's right, y'all — the mugger said proudly.

— He just called you a peckerwood too! — Vic stated the glaring contradiction.

— Who cares! — said the Light one—. This gentleman is absolutely right! He should be able to do anything he wants because of the sad history his people have suffered.

— No, he shouldn't. His Window World history isn't even his. Didn't you all learn human time periods without even living them? Black History has nothing to do with it.

— If you believe that, then you really are a racist!

— Let's get something clear. I'm not a racist. I just think a person is defined by one's actions. If you're a mugger, then you're a piece of shit. Regardless of history or skin color. Nor does history or skin color allow you to get away with bad things.

— Don't listen to him, sir — said the Light one to the Dark one ignoring the alien —. You can take my car, my clothes, my life in blood dollars... anything you want! I only have two cell phones, though. Can you please let me keep one?

— That's cool — said the Dark one —. For this time, dawg. Unless you racist as well?

— NO, NO, NO. Of course not! I can give you my home too! But please let me keep one phone!

— How's 'bout this? I'll take everything you're offering me, including your racist motherfucking life, and I'll collect the second phone once I cap yo light ass in a month. A'ight?

— Deal! But please let me keep my phone and stop believing I'm a racist! I swear I'm not. I'M NOT!

— You better recognize, dawg!

— Un-fucking-believable — Vic said to himself.

— But first we gonna cap this peckerwood racist motherfucker! — added the mugger.

— Neither of you are a match for my powers. Don't waste your breath.

— I meant in social media. That's real murder, boyyyyyy!

— Cool it — said a voice from behind —. This cat's with me.

Vic turned around and there was a stout Dark Blue Crystal Man wearing a hat, sunglasses, a colorful jacket and neck chains on the driver's seat of a Cadillac Convertible.

— Daaaaamn! — said the mugger —. You friends with Mister Ray? Then everything's filthy y'all!

PLAY

The mugger offered to bump his fist. Vic did so rolling his eyes and giving him a mild electric shock. The mugger cringed but didn't utter a word. Instead, the Light and Dark one proceeded to look at their cell phones. They became tech zombies with wide eyes and faces like the rest of the flock. The Grunge Rock Alien entered the Cadillac while he looked suspiciously at the Black Hole Sun.

END SIDE 1. TAPE SWITCH. SIDE 2.
PLAY

SPOONMAN

Vic Grunge drove with the mystery man for a while without speaking. His eyes were fixated on the sky's weird behavior.

— So? — Ray asked faintly—. No chit chat?

STOP

— What? — Vic asked—. Did you say something?

— A thank you would be nice.

— Yeah, thanks. I'm sorry. I just have a lot on my mind.

— It's cool. You're probably wondering about the sky. Sad the mountain ain't out today. Or every day for that matter.

— Forecast calls for a Black Hole Sun?

— Liquid Sunshine as always.

— Whatever it is, it sucked up all the droplets. I feel the sky is manipulating everybody. Somehow related to cell phones.

— Hope it'll burn off. Black Silence is doing this. Took the Big Dark to a whole other level. Linked his tech to some sort of brainwashing device.

— So, you're here to help me against the person who was supposed to help me?

— Straight up.

— Why?

— Why not? Is it so inconceivable I want to save the city as much as you do?

— Because you're blue? No race pun intended.

— That racial PC shit is part of his plan, man. Though I can't prove anything nor have the powers to face him. That's why I need you.

— Fair enough. So, what do we do?

— I can only give you information, cat.

— All right, let's start with the Cicadas. What's the deal?

— Those damn bugs have been around since the beginning of time. Actually ate Deaf Metal. Somehow Black Silence potty-trained them to be his bitches. Police officers that can fine you only for jaywalking. It's rumored he used the metal for leverage. But my theory is it has to do with the manipulation that's going on all around. Maybe sound related due to their sudden "Hush" quality.

— They sang before?

— Like you wouldn't believe. The Blue Zone was a noisy area until Black Silence put an end to it.

— You know "hummina, hummina" is a sexual innuendo where I come from.

— Be glad they're not trying to mate with you then.

— So where do I fit in this whole scenario?

— Your recent arrest gave Black Silence more ideas. Music has been reinstated. But now it's mandatory to wear earphones when you hear songs on your cell phone. They were manufactured instantly. Hush Cicadas have been scattered to enforce their use. People are listening to music again. Yet those without earphones, get their phone smashed in front of them by the Fuzz. It already started to happen.

— Let me guess... before the phone-smashing, they say, "You have the right to remain silent!" in Hummenese.

— Oh snap.

They both laughed. Ray halted at a stoplight and Vic started looking at the citizens on the street. Those who weren't wearing earphones, got their phones destroyed in front of them by the Hush Cicadas. Most of them were listening to Bad Bunny. One of them was surrounded by women with giant asses.

— On the other hand — Vic continued —, that's a law I can agree with. Especially when it comes to assholes playing shitty music without any disregard for the rest of the community. As much as I hate to admit it, I side with Black Silence on this one.

— You think? — Ray asked rhetorically.

— Though this action would still compromise his mind manipulation plans.

— Bligga, please. How much time do you think an average citizen could live without a phone?

— Good point. Just saw this dude earlier literally bargaining his life for one. I guess watching reels about a rapping baby has become more important than actually being born.

— You like hip hop?

— I have more of a Gangsta Rap personality.

— Well, I'm going to be a hip hop rapper.

— What are you gonna sing about?

— You see those women over there. BABY GOT BACK!!! There's a song in there somewhere.

— Being all of you made of Crystal, why not PUT'EM ON THE GLASS?

— Hey that's good, cat! May I keep that?

— It's always been yours. So, where are we headed?

— I was waiting for you to see the Patches hologram.

— You mean the clown? What about him?

— Legend says only you could see the code. But I'm the one who knows the person that can decipher it.

— Who is it?

— He's called the Spoonman. It may sound kinda crazy, but he can decipher any encrypted code in an alphabet soup. I have one in the foam cup in the back seat.

— Isn't everything you eat here basically soup?

— I was really expecting some sarcastic comment regarding the Spoonman.

— After the Hush Cicadas, nothing surprises me right about now.

— I can see that — the rapper said parking the Cadillac —. We're here. This is where we part ways. Please save our city. You're our only hope.

— You can count on it, Ray. Thanks again for your help.

— Spoonman is down that alley, cat. Don't forget the soup.

Vic got out of the car and took the foam cup. He went down the alley as instructed and found a Light Blue Man sitting on the floor in a yoga lotus position. His eyes were closed as if meditating. Soon after, he opened them and got on his feet to greet the superhero.

— You must be the Grunge Rock Alien — the Spoonman stated getting out an arsenal of spoons.

— I am — Vic responded.

— Open the soup and put it in front of me. Also tell me the letters you saw.

— Here you go — the alien said opening the alphabet soup in front of him—. The letters were D, D, O, E, D, L, P, S and A.

— You can listen to your music if you want. I must do my thing.

— Your thing?

— Kind of like a rain dance.

— If you say so.

PLAY

Vic took a few steps back and watched the great Spoonman perform his unique silverware dance. His many spoons clicking harmonically while he jumped and spun like a top with great ability. The rhythm blended with nature itself. At the same time, inducing hunger in some sort of Pavlovian association of utensil clunking before a meal. The alien would definitely eat the soup after the ritual since he could hear everything over the other spoons in his own music.

Rain came pouring down and then sucked back into the black hole. In sync with all the literal metal music spawned by the virtuous street performer. The Spoonman then came to a sudden stop and dunked one of the spoons in the soup. He kneeled and invited Vic to see. The alphabet soup now spelled the words "DOD PEDALS." So clear, yet so confusing. What did it all mean?

LIMO WRECK

Vic said goodbye to the Spoonman and walked out of the alley. He thought only about eating the soup. But then, a white limousine drove by at high-speed trying to run him over. The alien quickly took evasive action doing a 360-back-flip in the air and summoning a lightning bolt to break his fall. Though avoiding death once again, the soup spilled to the ground. And the limo just kept driving away.

— AH, HEEEEEEELLL NO! — Vic said with chest-bubbling rage.

The alien started tailing the limousine swinging atop his bolt vines. As he got closer, the limo's sunroof opened. A Fat Cat Light Blue Crystal Person emerged with a machine gun (he literally was fat and had an anime cat mask on). The Blue Man started shooting at Vic while laughing in an insane manner. Opportunely, Vic had electromagnetism at his disposal and could stop the bullets from ever reaching his body. The problem was the sheer volume of ammunition shot at him. With no time to reverse them to their origin. The superhero had to multitask swinging from the lightning while generating short magnetic forcefields to drop the bullets to the ground. He even tried controlling the limousine itself. But for some reason, it was not possible. Vic realized the internal combustion engine was diesel and it could not be controlled. All the while, the Fat Cat switched weapons after running out of bullets. Aside from the machine gun, Vic had to endure shots being fired by two Uzis, an AK-47 and a bazooka. To that adding some innocent bystanders that were run over by the driver.

This last part was what really made him angry. Not to mention the rocket that destroyed the top of the Columbia Center with some civilian casualties. Vic personally hated a life wasted on somebody else's irresponsibility. Even more so when a historical landmark was tampered with. Though the limo couldn't be controlled, other vehicles could be manipulated. As luck would have it, a Tesla dealership was nearby.

Vic started a lot of engines and crashed the cars directly into the limo one after the other. The driver lost control of the vehicle by the fifth car and crashed into a wall. He was dead upon the alien's arrival. The Fat Cat lay injured on the sunroof. Vic levitated him by his neck chains and let him fall at his feet.

STOP

— HAVE YOU LOST YOUR FUCKING MIND! — Vic screamed in anger.

— I'm rich! — the Fat Cat replied with a dying voice —. I'm immortal... I CAN DO WHATEVER THE FUCK I WANT!

— Yeah, like dying. All the riches in the world won't change that. Everybody dies. Death makes no exception for richer or poorer. Take it from somebody who's dead inside. And not by choice.

— YOU UNDERPRIVILEGED FUCK! YOU KNOW WHO I AM? WHO MY FATHER IS? YOU CAN'T TOUCH ME!

— Wrong. Say hi to the other rich assholes in the afterlife.

— FUCK YOU!

Vic exploded the Fat Cat by means of electricity without feeling remorse of any kind. Crystals shattered and the anime head rolled to his feet. Silence surrounded him while perceiving the rich man's corpse. He fled the scene just when a bystander stopped to watch. A regular citizen listening to Bad Bunny without earphones. A Hush Cicada flew down and destroyed his phone.

PLAY

THE DAY I TRIED TO LIVE

Though secretly enjoying the Fat Cat's execution, Vic was deeply troubled after this incident. Not really in a Bipolar way, since his chest was not exactly radioactive at the time. But playing the hero started to get tedious. And sometimes things could go terribly wrong like with the Mailman. An event that still plagued him from the inside. He only wanted a normal life. To pretend at least. To be... like them. Careless. Trivial. Free. And no responsibilities whatsoever. Throwing in the towel was the right thing to do. Live his life without any attachments or commitments of any kind. He didn't care anymore. Being a superhero was not all it was cracked up to be. Superpowers aside, everything sucked. It wasn't about glory or being loved. It was about making sacrifices that nobody cared about. Why even bother then?

Vic took off his flannel and threw it in the trash. The Grunge Rock Alien was no more. He started walking and went into a George and Dragon Pub without a worry in the world. The alien ordered a liquid burger basket and asked for a Vitamin R or a schooner of any brand (though they gave him a non-alcoholic beer for being under age). Nonetheless, Vic consumed his food and beverage anxiously. Not so much because of the tasty drops. Or because of his hunger. Which he was used to. But because of the people around him.

Even trying to conform left him in the freak spotlight. An alien fighting hopelessly to fit in. Like he didn't belong there at all. Though the place itself was very nice, it was a sports bar. And most of the people there were sport fans. Something he knew very little about outside the 90s era. Not to mention that sports history on Earth had little to do with the actual sports going on in Window World. In that moment, Vic really felt that he was from another planet. Not knowing how to behave or strike a conversation with any of them.

Imitation was his only social weapon. And there was a group of jocks and cheerleaders to try it on. He paid in blood dollars and approached the women.

STOP

— Anyways, girlfriend — a hot Crystal Cheerleader said to another —, I was like in SoDo and he was like "Me?" and I was like "Duh!" and he was like "Hmm?" and I was like "Pfff!" and he was like "Huh?" and I was like "Nuh-uh" and he was like "Okay!" and I was like "Looooser!"

— Excuse me — Vic said in a shy voice —. Your conversation sounds so... interesting. Can you elaborate?

— "Elaborate"? What are you a geek?

— HEY! — a Light Blue jock screamed grabbing Vic by the shirt and slamming him against the wall—. You talking to my girl?

— YES, BUTCH! — the cheerleader shouted—. AND HE SAID HE WOULD EAT MY PUSSY!

— NO, I DIDN'T! — Vic barked disturbed by the lie.

— Then what do you want, smart ass? — Butch continued with his army of jocks behind him.

— I wanted to... you know... talk sports.

— Oh! You want to talk sports, do you?

— I swear.

— Okay, I'll ask you a bunch of questions. For every answer you get wrong, I punch you in the face. Seem fair?

— Questions about what?

— General sports trivia.

— 90's sports trivia from Earth?

— Nope.

— You know what? I'll save you the trouble. You can kick the living shit out of me. Won't get anything right outside of my comfort zone anyways.

— My pleasure.

PLAY

The jock started punching Vic until he fell to the ground. The other jocks continued to kick him as he squirmed on the floor. All the while the alien wished to be back in his spaceship... never having left in the first place. But that wasn't the worst part. After being thrown out and Vic returned to the same garbage can, his blue flannel shirt was gone!

KICKSTAND

The powerless superhero looked around in all directions and quickly noticed a surge of electricity coming from the street. Specifically, a biker gang with similar cat helmets like the one used by the deceased limo nut. He managed to see the name in the back of one of the cuts which read, "Hell's Kittens." Just being reminded of the Fat Cat made his chest boil. Shortly after, Ray appeared once again. This time on a Harley with a dog mask over his head instead of a hat.

STOP

— Hop on, Vic! — Ray said with a smile —. We'll catch up to those assholes.

— Really appreciate that, Ray — Vic said sitting in the back.

— It wasn't very smart what you did with your Seattle tux.

— Trust me. I'm never taking the flannel off again. I just got an epiphany that it's fucking awesome not to belong.

— That's filthy. Now let's get these fuckers.

— Dog mask?

— Dogs chase cats, don't they?

— I suppose they do, Ray. I suppose they do.

PLAY

Ray put his dog mask on and accelerated the bike to full speed. The Hell Kittens weren't very far up ahead but they had to move quickly. In between cars, jumping red lights and thrusting through slanted terrain. This drew the attention of many Hush Cicadas that started to tail them. Luckily, Ray had street smarts and used dark alleys to lose them. In fact, the rapper's driving skills were so good, it only took a minute to find the bikers.

STOP

The Hell Kittens slowed down and turned around to confront them. Vic and all the bikers got off their motorcycles. Their Biker Leader was wearing Vic's blue flannel shirt and a Japanese kitty mask with large fangs. His cut was tied to his waist. The Grunge Rock Alien told his friend to leave since he already had a plan and Ray might be held accountable for the resulting effects. Once the rapper left, the Biker Leader approached the alien pompously.

— Look who it is — said the Hell Kitten leader raising his mask.

— Give me back my shirt — Vic replied with a mad look in his eyes.

— Oh, you want your tuxedo? No problem. I can return it if you give me back something you stole from me.

— What's that?

— My son. Can you bring him back from the dead?

— I'm sorry about your son. But he had it coming for shooting at me and the entire city. Killing innocents in the process. The limo driver also ran over many people. Even tried to run me over. Fucking asshole didn't know how to drive.

— That's normal here. You get used to it after a while. As for my son, I admit he was a hothead. Always trying to live a life of luxury on my money with no consequences. You're probably right. But he's still my son. And you must die for what you did. It's only fair that I kill you with the same superpowers you took for granted!

— I thought bikers were tough guys. Extreme macho types. The very depiction of real men.

— You're not helping your case if you're suggesting the opposite. I am a real man! That's why I'm called SABRETOOTH MONSTER COCK!

— Whoa. You kiss your mother with that nickname? From your mask alone I can infer Sabretooth Monster Cock is Hello Kitty's white trash cousin.

— White?

— Oh, sorry. Light Blue trash cousin.

— What the fuck does that even mean?

— I mean that if you're a real man, you would face me without the powers. And with none of your lackeys intervening.

— Sounds reasonable. You're gonna get pounded either way. The bruises you have now tell me that you got your ass handed to you recently. And I've been brawling on the street since I was your age. YOU'RE GOING DOWN!

— Two more things.

— What's that?

— First, put on some fighting music. I don't have any good fight songs in my playlist.

Sabretooth Monster Cock stared at him for a moment in silence. He took off the blue flannel shirt and threw it on the ground. Though being a middle-aged man, Sabretooth had a body builder figure with fur and veins popping out of his glass skin... just like his name implied... a nice big extinct feline cock. The Biker lowered his mask and proceeded to play "Any way you want it" by Journey on his phone at full volume. Vic looked at him funny. Particularly because this is what Sabretooth Monster Cock considered "ass kicking" music.

But he didn't need to laugh about it. Since his plan all along was for him to take off the shirt and be as loud as possible. Something that would alert the Hush Cicadas. Which, in fact, drew them there immediately. One of them smashing Journey into oblivion while seven others cuffing all the bikers. The reason being Ray's previous pursuit was pinned entirely on them. While Vic was let go for not owning a bike and using his headphones. The born-again superhero picked up his flannel shirt, dusted it with his hand and put it on with a smirk on his face. A blueish glow emanated briefly from his body like an aura of electrical power. Cuffed and escorted by the Cicadas, Sabretooth turned to the Grunge Rock Alien.

— Very clever — the Biker Leader admitted.

— That's my real muscle — Vic said with confidence —. My brain. I only fucked up taking off the flannel, trying to be normal and falling in love with a Nazi.

— A Nazi?

— Feminist Nazi to boot.

— How that work out for ya? Did she brand your balls with the Star of David?

— That's just plain nasty. But let's say everything was Louder than Love. I learned my lesson though. That's what wisdom really is. Getting fucked over so you can tell everybody to fuck off. So fuck off, pussycat.

— I'm curious. What was the second thing?

— Oh, another piece of advice — Vic said levitating his hands and taking all the bike's kickstands with magnetic powers—, it's the little things that matter, Monster Cock.

All the bikes fell to the ground at the same time. Sabretooth Monster Cock through a fit of rage as did the rest of the cuffed bikers.

— YOU PIECE OF SHIT! — Sabretooth Monster Cock screamed with vein-popping wrath—. NOW I'M GONNA TORTURE YOU TO DEATH! ONCE I MAKE BAIL, I'M FASHIONING A NEW BIKE OUT OF YOUR CARCASS AND MY SON'S HEADSTONE WILL BE POLISHED WITH YOUR ENTRAILS!

— It's a date, Sugar Fangs — the alien said mocking him—. But only if you promise you'll have "Don't stop believing" playing in the background.

The Biker leader growled. Vic smiled at him and fled the scene swinging from his lightning bolt vines.

PLAY

FRESH TENDRILS

But his victory would be short lived. Just as the alien used electromagnetism on the kickstands, somebody was using magnets on him. Ironically, with the blue shirt he had put on. Vic was dragged on his back in mid-air and at high speed for at least a mile. Stopping and getting caught in a pink plasma web generated by the Seattle Gum Wall. His powers were frozen and there was little room to maneuver. While the alien was reflecting over what had happened, he saw a huge mechanical spider moving towards him through the web. Vic started to struggle and tried to use his powers again. But it was all hopeless. The spider webbed him up in cables and placed its two AC plug fangs in between his head. Moments after, an electrical shockwave ignited his skull. Vic screamed in pain. A different type of pain. He wasn't actually being electrocuted. Quite the opposite. It was more like being drained. As before being born. Conscious as a fetus. Clinging to mom's womb like a tendril. Fresh, but somehow, knowing what a terrible life it's going to be. Full of mistakes and regrets. A long time to be born and a long time to die. Life is not short if you think about living. If you want to die, but can't. Little did he know, that this played a bigger part in the rest of the city.

The last part of Black Silence's plan was set in motion. Everybody linked to a cell phone was now being brainwashed and controlled entirely. To what purpose? It was still a mystery. But Vic had bigger problems on his hands. The spider was killing him little by little. And being drained didn't affect whatsoever the radioactivity in his chest. So, whoever was doing it, knew perfectly well what they were doing. But then, the epiphany. The code. The enigmatic code. The DOD Pedals.

With the little electrical powers in his body, the alien could sense a guitar shop where the pedals were showcased in the window. If he could somehow harness enough lightning to turn them all on at the same time, the resulting effect would create a Feedback Bomb and cancel the force that was binding him. There was no need for a cable to connect pedal to amp. Both could be synched at will. Vic noticed the beacons creating the force field were made of Deaf Metal and would not withstand a sound of that magnitude. Also, that the reason his powers were restrained had to do with the fact that the rubber in the gum was disrupting the current in his flannel shirt. But there was a disgusting perk that could be used to his advantage. The saliva contained in each gum ball was a conduit for his electricity. All he had to do was generate an electric charge by hovering the liquid in each gum to contain a temporal net of his own that would enable him to use his powers for that particular task. And the Lightning Bearer did just that. First summoning the great one.

— WITH GREAT POWER, COMES GREAT FUCKING FEEDBACK — Vic screamed at the top of his lungs—. OH KIM THAYIL! GIVE ME GREAT POWER!

The Feedback Bomb was unleashed. Escalating all the pedals until the amps reached a high pitch able to release him from the digital web. As an added bonus, it would also affect the Hush Cicadas.

4TH OF JULY

Now free from the web, he destroyed the spider with a swift lightning bolt. This caused all the mind control to go away while the Blue People reflected on what went on in that short time. Vic continued to walk through Post Alley and leaped into the air where something caught his eye by the Waterfront. Fireworks started to fill the sky and the origin appeared to be the Seattle Great Wheel. As he landed in front of an empty parking lot in front of Miner's Landing, the alien contemplated all the firecrackers go up in smoke and loud bangs of fluorescent lights. Somehow, all this didn't appear as a joyful occasion. It reminded him of war and destruction. The Apocalypse... the End. It wasn't a big deal to him. In fact, why would his grungy nature not celebrate death?

But there was something more. Some type of mind control. Though it wasn't controlling him. Only altering his perceptions of reality. Making everything blurry. Like the fabric of what dreams are made of. And not in the good sense. Two men appeared before him. A Native American wearing a red shirt and a Blonde Conservative wearing a black shirt with jeans. The first one had powers of his own and started to jump in midair whirling moon beams at him from a lunar tattoo on his palm. The second one had a shotgun that fired tiny suns which would explode upon contact.

Vic Grunge took evasive action. Using lightning to swing, magnetism to shield himself and mechanical control to place as obstacles for his rivals. There was never any time to attack. The alien could only defend himself. But from who? The characters were human, but didn't make much sense. Maybe just as archetypes. Was he fighting the American dream? After clashing with the patriotic distortions and noticing only his chest bubbling from the fight, he realized the source of that bizarre display came from waves in the moving Ferris

Wheel. Vic finally attacked with a lightning bolt and struck the wheel itself right down the middle.

Both characters disappeared suddenly. Vic perceived that, in some strange way, the conflict was with himself. The two opponents that ambushed him were distortions of his own identity. He was an American. An alien in a different planet. But still an American. Pieced together from everything that made his former country great. But also, the celebration of war. Him being a warrior in that battle. The one who brought peace by tearing the world to shreds for an ideal. The ideal called Freedom. What purpose was there to live in peace when nobody was free? The end of the world. In a blink of an eye. Without freedom, it was already over. That was the American dream.

HALF

As Vic found new meaning in his life, the undamaged Ferris Wheel turned horizontally with a person hovering on top. It was an African American dressed in black corduroy and blue stainless-steel shoulder pads, belt and boots. He had a blue mohawk, wore visor Y2K sunglasses and sported a lot of gold chains and rings. The Seattle Great Wheel started to turn clockwise and moved towards the Grunge Rock Alien. Aside from this, all the bikers he thought were in prison came out from inside, above and around Miner's Landing. It was obvious they didn't just make bail, but that their services were retained. Most probably not even paid given their need to escape some jail time or the whole gang's vendetta against the alien. The Hush Cicadas were strangely absent.

Vic swung around their leader and started to throw lightning bolts from his palms. But he was protected by some sort of force field. It was connected to the same Ferris Wheel that could also spring many weapons. The alien was struck in the air by a flow of liquid metal controlled by the mysterious figure. Refined Deaf Metal which could not be controlled by his magnetic powers. Nor any of his contraptions for that matter. Vic fell to the ground with some cuts and bruises. But nothing serious. The man descended until hovering a few feet above the ground. Knowing he was out of his league, the superhero got up and decided to take a different approach.

STOP

— Don't tell me — Vic asked with his classic acid humor—, Space Mister T?

— It's Black Silence, bitch! — the supervillain responded arrogantly.

— I was kind of hoping you'd say, "I PITY THE FOOL WHO LOVES MUSIC!"

— Music ain't gonna save yo' cracker ass this time. I'm sure you can recognize a worthy foe when you see one. You seem eager to know how I fucked you up, bitch.

— First, I'm still standing. So, you haven't won yet. Second, stop calling me "bitch."

— But that's what you are. You're my little bitch, aren't you? I used you from the start. Yo' powers only helped fuel my Black Hole. Which also served to divert attention from the mind control I harnessed from your electricity, you know what I'm saying?

— I can see everything except the Feedback Bomb. You weren't keen on that, you narcissistic fuck. That was me making you my bitch with noise smacking the shit out of your silence.

— You racist bitch! How can you say you're going to smack the shit out of my black ass! You can't say I'm black!

— I never did. I said SILENCE. Why is everybody in this planet so touchy? It's as if you're all made of... OH... I get it now!

— I ain't made of glass, bitch. Quite the opposite. And at first, I really wanted to be one of them. But the Crystal People couldn't look past the color of my skin. Yo' naive-ass dad made the mistake of sending a black man into a blue community. They were more racist than the fucking KKK! Which only pissed me off beyond words. Making my will as strong as the metals I would later forge to get even. With them... with you! The fucking cause of it all. Becoming a true Web-Footer, I managed to create lighter and darker blue citizens through my Black Hole tech. Only then would they understand!

— So, you introduced racism to stop racism? That's smart.

— You can't know! You're not black! You haven't been called a BLIGGER!

— Bligger? What the fuck...? Oh, I understand. Black is the darker shade of blue.

— YOU DISSING ME, BITCH??

— Nope, but I'll paint you a word picture. With 90's sports to honor those assholes from the bar. Michael Jordan and Larry Bird. Barry Sanders and Joe Montana. The motherfucking GOATs. You think it matters if they were black or white? Everybody keeps focusing on the wrong things. It's not about skin color. It's about excelling to greatness. Being all you can be. And in that field, we're all alike. All of us have a unique talent and anybody can go places with what they know. Actions know no race. And if by the color of your skin you find more obstacles, then you become even greater once you overcome them. Just complaining about it, well... that's what really makes you a pathetic little bitch.

— You mean you wouldn't be happier watching white people television in a white man's world?

— I grew up on Family Matters and Fresh Prince. Loved them both. Didn't need to be black to enjoy them. You could do the same.

— Funny you should mention that, bitch. That's how I created light and dark skins. Internet cookies based on user preference through cell phone reception. Tuning into specific black or white programs changed their brainwaves and I could reconfigure their DNA sequence entirely. Even the basic melanin genes that determine skin color. Yo' pop ain't the only genetic genius in Window World history, you know what I'm saying?

— You mean I would have been black in your world? Cool! Though I can't imagine having a larger dick than the one I have right now.

— Rather you stay white. Much easier to keep fucking you up.

— Now who's being racist?

— You still don't get it.

— Get what?

— Where you ever shunned? Outcasted? Forced into a life where you had to join lesser beings?

— The A-Team?

— NO! The Cicadas, you dumb bitch! I taught them the English language and pretty soon they saw me as their leader. I was very fond of technology and experimented a lot on Deaf Metal. I noticed that everything has a frequency. Much like a radio station, I can tune in and change the songs in everybody's head, you know what I'm saying? Reconfiguring DNA strands themselves to whatever the fuck I want. How's that for excelling?

— It's admirable. But you're still doing it for the wrong reasons. Seeking revenge on racist assholes makes you even more of a racist asshole. You must commit entirely. Heck, even half would be something to hope for. But with nothing but empty hands... I bet your final plan is to only keep the dark blue people alive.

— Damn right!

— Then what? You don't think conflicts can arise within the same race?

— Not after I'm done brainwashing them to my image. No more Blue People. Draining your energy has given me the power to eliminate choice, you know what I'm saying? Now, like the skies, they will all choose the one and only option: BLACK!

— A city full of narcissists has a population of one. And that's one too many. I should thank you for the Black Hole Sun, though. It finally sucked in the goddamn Seattle rain.

— What are you a pussy? It was just some low-level sleet.

— Why not turn it off then?

— You must really think I'm stupid.

— Oh yeah. I do. But not because of this. I think you're stupid because you stole music from these people. That's the very essence of Being. Calling yourself "Silence" makes you even more of a dumbass.

— I can control thoughts. Not emotions. And music awakens emotions, you know what I'm saying? I would lose control of the fucking heard. And I'm the dumbass.

— Oh, but you are. You have revealed your true weakness. So, all I have to do to beat you, is raise a boom box in the air?

— Not quite, bitch — Black Silence said taking out his Blue Dot Speaker—. You see, I do love to hear a lot of motherfucking songs. But surely it's not the type of tunes that you chill to. Doom Orb... PLAY TRAP MUSIC!!!!

— Holy shit rusting me — Vic expressed to himself in repulsion.

— YO BIKERS... GET THAT, BITCH!

Trap Music started playing intensely. Aside from weakening him and stealing his powers, the uncoordinated beats in the music were throwing off his game. And the Hell Kittens were already pouncing towards him in lynch mode. Sabretooth Monster Cock had dibs on drawing first blood. But Vic Grunge was much smarter than he appeared to be. He was right on calling Black Silence on the Feedback Bomb. The supervillain really had no idea. And the alien knew this because he had another card up his sleeve.

Vic never stopped thinking about the Feedback Bomb's effect on the Cicadas. His first theory was that they were just scared. But, in reality, it only broke the connection like it did with the gum web. The same way it liberated the Blue People from his mind control. For them, it would appear to be some sort of confused amnesia. However, if the Cicadas were to hear the same sound again, they would rush to see the culprit responsible. Before all this, Vic had linked the guitar pedal technology with ordinary electric timers. Pointed directly at Black Silence upon meeting him. So, when all the villains charged towards him in merciless wails, they couldn't understand his willingness to stand still. Soon all their doubts would be answered.

The second Feedback Bomb went off and all the Cicadas came flying in anger. They weren't dressed like cops. The giant bugs were completely naked as they were in nature. And as in nature, they started singing again. But not just any song. A chorus. A very loud chorus. Worse than the Feedback Bomb. Conveniently, Vic had his headphones in place and the Doom Orb was destroyed by the Cicada chant.

PLAY

LIKE SUICIDE

Grunge Rock was immune to the Cicada Symphony. This also benefitted the alien regarding his foes. The Hell Kittens started to crack while Black Silence was down on his knees covering his ears. One other weakness omitted in the conversation was that the supervillain had misophonia. It's not music specifically he hated, but noise in general. He was incredibly sensitive to it. And now all control was lost. Even his Big Wheel Tech was malfunctioning. As for the bikers, Vic's recycled energy from the spider had given him super-speed and he managed to turn the forty Hell Cats to broken glass in a matter of seconds. Though a part of him felt bad for Sabretooth Monster Cock losing his son, another part felt glad for putting him out of his misery. It was an easy win for him as well. Sometimes the hero forgot they were all made of glass. So, after taking them out, Vic Grunge approached Black Silence with a leer on his face.

STOP

— HEY, BLACK SILENCE! — Vic cried out.
— What? — Black Silence answered weakly.
— SHUT THE FUCK UP!!!

PLAY

The Grunge Rock Alien hit Black Silence incredibly hard. The Ferris Wheel broke beneath him and the villain fell to the ground. Moments before drifting into unconsciousness, Black Silence laughed, took out a small remote and pressed the only blue button there. He then fainted and remained that way. Lucky for Vic that he did. Since the effects of the blue button flared the Black Hole Sun into a crimson frenzy. Lasers came from its core and targeted the Cicadas. Not exactly killing them, but making them killers. The targets being all the Blue People!

Vic swung from building to building taking out as many bugs as humanly possible. He used bolts, fast punches, magnetism, machines and super speed to try and keep them at bay. But even with his Lightning powers, it wasn't enough. Their numbers were just too great. And the total civilian casualties outweighed the people he actually saved doing all that he could do. Vic also felt sorry for the Cicadas. They were being used and appeared to be a peaceful tribe before they met Black Silence. And it was in that compassion and remembering his sentiments for the Biker leader, that the tragic answer presented itself.

The solution wasn't to kill them. But to help them die. They were already dead. Whatever Black Silence did to the Cicadas, there was no going back. The supervillain had ruined them psychologically. Even after stopping the mind control. So instead of breaking the connection, a third Feedback Bomb had to be launched. This time adjusted to the frequency of the life energy Vic felt in them. That twisted energy that screamed for mercy. He just had to create the opposite pitch in the feedback. It had a specific tempo which needed the aid of a lot of metronomes to synchronize perfectly. Much like a great drummer had innately.

— MIGHTY MATT CAMERON! — Vic roared synchronizing the metronomes—. I SUMMON THEE FOR THIS BIBLICAL BEAT!

This action resulted in all the Cicadas going quiet and killing themselves. Like Suicide. A Cicada's suicide. Silence. Hence the villain and the Hush Cicadas. Those who only cried out for death, were now dead. At peace. Free.

TAPE STOPPED

Vic still managed to find one of the Cicadas uttering his last words. He kneeled, let his headphones hang from his neck and heard what the insect had to say.

— Hummina, hummina... hummina... Hummina, HUMMINA, HUMMINAAAA!!! — the Cicada said dying shortly after.

— AH FUCK! — Vic said to himself —. That sounded important. Alas, the legacy of a whole species dies with my ignorance.

Vic Grunge bowed his head in shame. He leaped to the skies and swung down to Black Silence's fainted body. The alien took his flannel shirt off and tied it around the clone's waist. The supervillain was imprisoned very much like his former love partner. But with Lightning restraints instead of Wind cuffs. Even having functional prisons in the Blue Zone, Vic couldn't take any chances. He contemplated the sky changing to its natural blue tone and the citizens returning to their regular lives. Ray appeared in his Cadillac and parked in front of him.

— You did it, cat! — the rapper cried out joyfully —. You saved us!

Vic looked around and witnessed everybody checking out their cell phones without giving him any credit for his heroism.

— Did I? — the alien asked sarcastically.

— Well— Ray answered—, it's still better than before.

— Tell that to the Cicadas. I just helped wipe out an entire species.

— You're kidding, right? They're bugs, man. They have like a billion kids in eggs alone. I've seen them with my own eyes. To that add millions in teenage larvae underground. All of them untampered by the mind manipulation of that piece of shit.

— That's good to know.

— Though I think Black Silence had another evil plan since some of them looked almost human. Not sure if they were cross-breeds or something even more sinister.

— Why am I not surprised.

— I'm pretty sure he manipulated me in some way to lure you to certain places. Note it wasn't intentional.

— That's cool, Ray. I'm used to being betrayed by now. Even by those who were not actually betraying me.

— That's sad, cat! In that case, you have any advice for me in the future?

— You know the clones have Doom Orbs that shut down my powers with shitty music?

— How is that advice?

— It's not. Just wanted to make sure you won't make music that will take away my powers.

— Asshole.

Both of them laughed. Ray opened the car door and Vic got in. He was driven back to the entrance where his mission had officially ended. But the alien still had two more missions waiting for him. Seattle was a mysterious place. In all its colors. And this city, she likes surprises. Like the Spoonman being elected president thanks to the impromptu elections imparted by the alien. Before exiting, the Alternative Valkyrie hologram appeared before Vic once again. The statue had some subtle differences, but it still had his mother's face. The superhero bowed down and confessed his debaucheries:

— Bless me Goddess, for I have sinned. I needed to bitch-slap the victim for siding with the mugger out of racial guilt. Had sexual urges with the big booty girls. Wanted to play soccer with the Fat Cat's head. Felt like returning to the sports bar Superman II style and kick the living shit out of all the jocks with my renewed superpowers. Maybe go to a karaoke bar and sing a Journey song in Hummenese. Thought "Fuck tha Police" every time I saw a Hush Cicada and wanted to call everybody a bitch after meeting Black Silence. Kinda grows on you.

MOMENTS LATER, ANOTHER paper came down from heaven with the word "Post" written on it. It rendered him unconscious as before.

PART THREE: ALICE IN CHAINS

The alien awoke in his ship like always. As he came to, Vic wondered if it was all a dream. A dream within a dream. Where one would wake up but never really did. There was a new purpose aside from the other ones. To wake up. And maybe the game had to end for that to happen. His eyes were fixated on his next tape. One with a woman buried in sand entitled *DIRT* by the band Alice in Chains. It made him think about the Alternative Valkyrie. Who was the mysterious figure? Did his father carve his mother's face for a specific reason? Was there any meaning behind the Celestial Fortune Cookies? Only time would tell.

The Grunge Rock Alien took out the Soundgarden tape and replaced it with AIC. Vic then proceeded to his closet and chose to wear the yellow flannel shirt. It was always an enigma to him what elemental powers would spawn from the enchanted garment. But this was only revealed once the specific zone was entered. Since the colors had to match, he travelled to the Yellow City by the south entrance.

PLAY

THEM BONES

Walking down the path, something scary and repulsive got in his way from the start. Bones. Human bones. Two hundred and six of them. Multiplied by a million. Replacing the dirt. Coming out of the dirt. Piling up on the side like walls. Was this a warning to turn back? Something curious about Bipolars is that they don't mind being put in harm's way. They don't fear death. Even want it deep down. But the fear of death wasn't what Vic felt in that precise moment. Just the realization that he wasn't a god. Nor anything special. Death would come to him too. Herein is life's final joke. Even if you're the most powerful Being in existence, the thought of dying makes you humble. And everybody dies. Like them bones. One day covered in living flesh, and suddenly, without any flesh at all. Gone. Empty. The meaning of life is to give those bones a purpose. Like fossils. An everlasting symbol. Immortality only exists in what we do. And the alien knew something worthwhile had to happen before his demise. At the end of the road, an anthropomorphic dog wearing a baggy top hat with stars, colorful clothes and white sunglasses was waiting for him. Surely the Yellow City's Sentinel.

STOP

— Well — the dog said switching to a singing tone —, if it isn't the GRUNGE... ROCK... ALIEOOOON!

— That's a first — Vic said sarcastically —. Let me take a wild guess here... your name is Dog?

— Star Dog, actually. South Road Sentinel, at your service.

— Right. Forgot about the hat.

— Great day, isn't it?

— You do realize we're surrounded by mountains of human bones?

— So?

— It's not really my idea of Paradise. I'm Bipolar but I'm not fucking Goth.

— Beauty is in the eye of the beholder. As a human, you see death. As a dog I see a whole lot of bones to scarf on. OH YEAAAAAH!

— True... didn't see it that way. Where did they come from?

— Them bones? Not sure. The Yellow City clone gave them to me as a gift.

— Big surprise.

— I sense mistrust in your voice.

— Let's just say I had very bad experiences with clones in general. I already know who the new supervillain is.

— He's actually a very nice guy. But don't take my word for it. I'm an extremely positive canine.

— So, you don't think that the Yellow People are assholes?

— Yes, of course they are. But getting upset about it would make me an asshole as well.

— I don't follow.

— Why is an asshole an asshole?

— Is this the riddle?

— No. Throwing around some Chocolate Starfish philosophy.

— That's fucking disgusting. And no idea.

— Because it's full of shit.

— Was that a joke?

— Maybe. But the fact is you're full of shit when you take in too much food. When you let those insults and basic misanthropy consume you from within. Then all you do is crap all over the world.

— This analogy is making me sick, Star Dog.

— Just pointing out why I love bones. Without food, there's no chance of being an asshole. YEAH MADAFAKA!

— Sure... can we move on to the riddle please?

— In due time. But before that... HAVE YOU EVER HEARD THE STORAAAAY?

— What story?

— STORAAAAAY!

— Fine. What STORAAAAAY?

— I see you haven't. That's disappointing. But it won't affect the outcome.

— Of what?

— Glory.

— You're not making any sense!

— Okay, the riddle. What happens when the Mothership loses its love?

— I'm done trying to find logic in these puzzles or even criticizing them. I'll just go for the answer this time. Since the Mothership must be a machine and lost love fucks you up, I'm going to say that it suffers some sort of a MALFUNCTION.

— CORRECT! Love is what makes the world go round, biatch! You can't be on my motherfucking mothership if you can't bring some motherfucking love.

— You're talking about the bones again, aren't you?

— Obviously!

— Figures. Can I go in now?

— Sure thing. It was nice to make your acquaintance, Vic Grunge. Hope I see you again IN THE MOOOORNIIIIING!!!

— Not likely. Have a nice day, Star Dog.

PLAY

DAM THAT RIVER

Vic entered the Yellow City. But, like in his former quest, his expectations of that place were completely the opposite in real life. It was a city in ruins. An Apocalyptic Dystopia. As if Seattle was nuked ten years ago. Aside from the chaos and destruction all around, there were absolutely no Crystal People whatsoever. Streets, buildings, and businesses were empty. And it felt even more silent than the Blue City. His yellow flannel shirt started glowing which meant his new superpowers were activated. He stretched out his hand to see what they were. And the only result was making a flower come out of the ground.

STOP

— Earth powers — Vic said disappointed —. That's swell.

— TAKE THAT! — a human man in a gold cap and brown jumpsuit screamed out while hitting him in the head with a coffee table.

— WHAT THE FUCK, MAN! — Vic complained with rage even though not seriously injured.

— Sorry — the mystery man responded in remorse—. My bad. I thought you were one of them.

— Them?

— Zombies. City's full of them.

— Nazi robots, Cicada Cops and now Post Apocalyptic Zombies? This shit keeps getting better and better.

— I'm the leader of the survivor resistance. All the Crystal People are stationed underground. I can take you there if you want.

— You're the clone, right?

— Yes. Call me Mister H.

— That's the thing. I don't trust clones. Least of all one calling himself "Mister

H."

— Really? Why is that?

— Well, the two former supervillains in my life were clones. So, I assume that all clones are evil until proven otherwise. And hitting me with a coffee table wasn't exactly a blowjob.

— Please. We need you. I need you. Contrary to your prior experiences, I do maintain my purpose to help the Grunge Rock Alien reach his.

— And what's my purpose?

— Find a solution for all the zombies, rebuild the city, escape the earth's core, reestablish the economy, politics, businesses... take your pick.

— Sorry, dude. Not following you.

— As you wish. But zombies will find you wherever you hide.

— I rather take my chances with them than with you. Besides, I have superpowers. Don't really need your help.

— At least let me cure your wound.

— What wound?

— Your neck is bleeding. A mild cut really.

— So that's what that sting is. And you were the one who made it bleed, FYI.

— That's why I want to help. I just need to apply some pressure on it.

Mister H put his thumb over his neck to block the blood flow. Vic flinched when the clone touched him. As if his mistrust was tattooed in his DNA. Mister H took his hand off and the wound was closed.

— There you go — Mister H said with a charming smile—. Your river has been dammed.

— Wow! — Vic said amazed —. It doesn't hurt anymore! And I actually feel much better!

— I'm glad. I'll leave you alone now. Good luck!

— Wait... I'll go with you. You look like a stand-up guy. Star Dog vouched for you so I think it would be wise to tag along.

— That's filthy! You won't regret it! Please follow me.

PLAY

Vic and Mister H walked through the uninhabited Yellow City. They strolled for a while through the sandy desert roads of the waste-ridden ruins of civilization. Mixed with the constant Seattle precipitation, the texture was pure Sludge. Vic started to fear what was behind all this silent chaos. Mostly where his mysterious guide was taking him and the zombies who were dormant for the time being. Though this calm scenario wouldn't last long.

RAIN WHEN I DIE

The cloudy sky started to roar with thunder. As they turned from short alley ways into 34th Avenue in Magnolia, Vic Grunge and his apocalyptic chaperon came across a horde of zombies. They were in fact Yellow Crystal People but they had missing limbs and were mostly cracked or shattered. Crystal zombies were devoid of liquid and, therefore, were attracted to any liquid they saw (normal Crystal People, humans, clones, animals, etc.) Since all the Yellow People took shelter underground, the zombies survived mainly on rain water. But today they had a tasty dish in front of them. And they would stop at nothing to drink the liquid that would satiate their torment. The zombies weren't slow either. They ran like Usain Bolt on energy drinks. Vic used his new superpowers to try and stop them. Pulling them to the ground, creating earth walls, summoning vines to wrap them up and stoning them with every mineral on the ground. Mister H took out some of them as well. But there were just too many of them. The only option was to run. Which they did… at maximum speed.

Nonetheless, the zombies were faster and eventually caught up with them. When realizing this, the Grunge Rock Alien levitated a large piece of the earth and flew around on it like a giant asteroid. Mister H was with him along with several zombies. They attacked as if trying to cut them with their sharded hands. Vic summoned a tree from the ground and shot sharp sticks simultaneously with accurate precision to shatter them all through the head… always through the head. This information came to him while attacking others on the ground. The shattered part of them would later reconfigure as if nothing happened. Therefore, the headshot was a must. But they were safe now.

STOP

— So — Vic said while thrusting forward with his giant piece of land —, where to?

— Head west towards the Washington Park Arboretum— Mister H answered.

— Gotcha. I think it's gonna rain.

— When you die…

— Sorry?

— When you die and become a zombie, liquid is the only way to survive. Rain is the living dead thirst quencher. That's why they all came out just now.

— Oh, couldn't care less. I can't stand the rain. Are there no fucking umbrellas in this stinking planet?

— What are you a pussy? It's just a little drizzle.

— So, I've been told. Can I ask you something?

— Shoot.

— What's the "H" stand for? Is it for "Hero"?

— Something like that.

— You have an embarrassing name or something? Don't tell me… Hanson, right?

— No, I just think letters are more powerful than words. You know that the letter "H" is silent in Spanish?

— Why use it then?

— Something maybe beautiful because it's hidden. Once exposed, it loses its magic.

— That sounds more like madness.

— How so?

— Not knowing something is there to later find out that it is. It's like living in an illusion and getting dick-slapped in the face with reality.

— What if the hidden element is a good thing?

— Sorry, but to me, anything that's hidden is an illusion. And all illusions are lies. Can something good come out of lying?

— Depends on the truth you're trying to cover up. All my people underground have been fed with illusions. The best one of all: Hope. Without it, they would all be fucking gone.

— Maybe... or they would strap on a pair and fight for themselves knowing what's out there.

— It's not that simple. They're all sick with the zombie virus. Most of them are lying down in their beds. Once we see they're going to turn, we dispatch them to the surface.

— You never kill them?

— Where's the hope in that? — the clone said smiling—. Of course there are exceptions. Basic survival rules. Up here it's kill or be killed. It hurts me every time I rub them out. But I can't have the luxury of becoming one of them. I couldn't let my people down.

— I get what you're doing. But what if it's a lost cause?

— The only lost cause is giving up. I'm trying to find the cure. I need to search the surface world and somebody has to search underground.

— You're going to leave me down there?

— I can't access certain places due to my lack of powers. You have to trust me. I know it's hard with what has already happened to you. But I genuinely want to save them. They mean everything to me. And if for some reason I tricked you, you could easily escape with your Earth abilities. You have nothing to lose. So... do you trust me?

— I don't trust anybody anymore. Be that as it may, I will choose to do so... I genuinely believe you're a pleasant person.

— Yeah, I get that a lot. We're here.

PLAY

Vic parked his flying piece of land in front of the park entrance. It started to rain in that precise instant. For a while, the alien felt like somebody was calling his name. A girl. He could make out the words "I'M LOST!" over his music. Was it his imagination or was somebody asking for help? At that point neither would have surprised him. So many strange things had come his way. And he was already insane to rule out delusions.

DOWN IN A HOLE

Mister H led the alien through the park passing through the decadent scenario that once was vibrant with plant life. Soon they came across a giant hole in the ground. It was so dark, Vic couldn't see past the first few feet. A part of him still felt like the clone was deceiving him. But he was right about one thing. His Earth powers could save him if there was any foul play involved. They said their farewells inferring they would meet later underground. Vic summoned a Jack O' Lantern Mushroom from the soil. The diameter was enough for him to stand on its head. With his Earth powers, Vic could see the attributes in the hidden flora beneath him. Which, in this species of mushroom, was the ability to glow in the dark. Now the alien could partly see inside the hole where he was descending atop the toadstool elevator.

The girl's voice came to mind. His chest started to boil with angst. Mostly the realization that there could be no relationship with any woman. Not because of his bad experience with her Nazi ex-girlfriend. But because of the life he chose. A hero's life had no time for emotional attachments. Even more so if she wasn't a supervillain. Vic could risk putting the person he loved in danger. And, in a life of constant sacrifices, love would be the most important sacrifice of all. Communication is key to any relationship. And yet, after living with depression, his tongue was burnt, his teeth kicked in and he felt buried being born. The only communication was with himself. Where to channel lost love? Vic could no longer fly in this region. As if flying was a privilege denied by the Earth itself. Going down was the only option. He was already addicted to being down. And addicts dig a hole not realizing they can't get out until they look up. Maybe the problem wasn't the capability of getting out with superpowers. But not wanting to get out at all.

STOP

Vic came across a forest. A very peculiar forest where the trees had faces. All of them were sleeping. Except for one who was awakened by the mushroom light and suddenly clobbered him senseless with one of his branches. The tree then spoke to the alien with his loud voice.

— TIME TO WAKE UP, YOUNG MAN! — cried the Screaming Tree.

— Why are you yelling? — Vic said irritated getting out of his short coma.

— WHAT?

— WHY ARE YOU YELLING?

— YOU'RE YELLING TOO!

— BECAUSE YOU'RE FORCING ME TO!!!

— SORRY. WE GREW UP IN THE MAD SEASON. THE WEATHER THERE IS PURE DISTORTION. CAN'T HEAR VERY WELL. SO, WE CAN'T CONTROL THE VOLUME IN OUR VOICE.

— WHY DID YOU HIT ME?

— I THOUGHT YOU WERE A LUMBERJACK COMING TO KILL US. WHY ELSE WOULD YOU WEAR THAT SHIRT?

— It's a Grunge thing.

— WHAT?

— NOTHING.

— NOTHING IS ALWAYS SOMETHING. WHEN NOTHINGNESS IS DEFINED, IT BECOMES SOMETHING. AND WHEN SOMETHING IS SOLVED, IT BECOMES PURPOSE.

— THAT'S GOOD! IS THAT FROM CONFUCIUS OR KANT?

— "CAN'T" IS NOT IN MY VOCABULARY. I ALWAYS BELIEVE THAT I CAN!

— I MEANT THAT THE GERMAN PHILOSOPHER... NEVER MIND! CAN I GO THROUGH?

— NOT UNTIL YOU ANSWER MY RIDDLE!

— NO, NO, NO! I ALREADY ANSWERED A FUCKING RIDDLE GETTING IN HERE!

— WELL, YOU HAVE TO ANSWER MINE IF YOU WANT TO CONTINUE INTO THE UNDERGROUND YELLOW CITY.

— WHAT IF I DON'T?

— ALL OF US WILL SCREAM AT YOU!!!!

— AAAAAAAH! — roared the rest of the trees waking up.

— STOP! — Vic said even more annoyed —. I'LL ANSWER YOUR RIDDLE. JUST SHUT THE FUCK UP!

— I NEARLY LOST YOU THERE — said the Screaming Tree he was speaking to.

— THE RIDDLE?!

— OH RIGHT! HERE GOES. WHAT'S THE ONLY THING THAT DOESN'T WASH AWAY WITH THE RAIN?

— Well, everything gets washed away eventually. Except the memory of getting washed away. So, I'm gonna say our memories.

— WHAT?

— MEMORIES!

— CORRECT! I ALSO WOULD HAVE ACCEPTED "THE SUMMER THAT ONLY I REMEMBER."

— WHY THE FUCK WOULD I ANSWER THAT?

— JUST SAYING!

— OKAY. MAY I PASS NOW?

— YES! YOU MAY GO... ABOVE!

— YOU MEAN BELOW!

— WHATEVER!

PLAY

And he did in fact go below. Down a series of steps that spiraled down with many torches on both flanks. And at the bottom, stood the beautiful human female who called to him.

SICKMAN

The girl was blonde, had blue eyes and was about the same age as him. She wore a black puffed sleeve dress with a white pinafore sported over the top with ankle-strap shoes. There were also chains over her shoulders and neck which appeared to be heavy and uncomfortable. At the time, she was picking red flowers from a small garden.

STOP

— ARE YOU OKAY? — Vic cried out.

— Why are you yelling at me? — the girl replied.

— Sorry. Force of habit when speaking to the trees.

— I know! They're so annoying!

— Tell me about it. What's your name?

— I'm Alice.

— Nice to meet you. I'm Vic.

— I know who you are. You're the Grunge Rock Alien.

— Where you the one calling me?

— Yes. Our Messiah believed you were not going to come down here so I gave you a little incentive.

— Damsel in distress?

— No such thing.

— You don't need me to free you from those chains then? Did the clone do this to you?

— I wrapped myself in these chains. I wouldn't have called him a Messiah if he did.

— And me and my ego thinking I was the Messiah. Why would you willingly wrap yourself in chains?

— You can only know freedom if you're not free. Once we find the cure, I will rid myself of these chains.

— I'm surprised you're human. Are you a clone too?

— To be honest, I don't really remember. But it's not important right now. Come... there's much I must show you.

PLAY

Alice started walking. Vic followed her pretty guide towards the entrance of the Yellow City. An extremely large cavern with high ceilings and several torches. It was full of beds and Yellow People lying sick in most of them. They were shivering, sweating and throwing up. Those who weren't sick, were praying to the several Mister H statues scattered throughout the cavern. After his ego joke, Vic wondered if the clone's ego was bigger giving the order to carve rock statues of himself. Or was it authentic religious admiration? Before he could answer his own question, one of them approached him wearing a minister uniform. He gave Vic a liquid Seattle Dog as an olive branch.

STOP

— Greetings, Earthling! — said the Yellow Priest giving him the hot dog—. We welcome you to the Church of H.

— Church of H? — Vic asked with suspicion—. This is not a cult, is it?

— Depends what you mean by "cult."

— Boy band purity rings and compelling me to commit suicide when you run out of truffle bars?

— Pardon me?

— My main concern being that you try to brainwash me and burn me at the stake if I don't turn.

— Certainly not! We accept different opinions. For instance, what God do you believe in?

— There's only one God and his name is Layne Staley.

— We were informed of another.

— Jerry Cantrell?

— Yeah no. Ours is called GRTB.

— Right. Mister H's love for letters. Do I dare ask what they stand for?

— We don't need to know.

— Clearly you don't.

— What do you mean?

— Something doesn't add up here.

— Are you questioning our faith? Even after I accepted your God LSJC?

— Please don't call them that. And I'm not questioning your faith. It just feels like you're being deceived... as am I... why am I here?

— DEMON!

— Sorry?

— YOU'RE A DEMON!!!

— Because I don't agree with you? Forcing your beliefs on somebody is not faith. It's a hunger for power and control. A cult. And cults only serve one master.

— You're speaking against our Messiah? OUR LORD?! The one who brought forth the aid cars of our souls?

— No, I'm speaking against idiots like yourself who blindly follow any dogma. And everybody who doesn't agree with you is a demon or goes to Hell. That's not religion. It's plain arrogance and the need to be right.

— IT IS HE! THE ONE WHO BRINGS THE PLAGUE. THE SICKMAN! LYNCH THE SICKMAN!

— What I wouldn't give for a Seattle Freeze right about now.

— RUN! — cried Alice.

— Yeah — Vic agreed —. Back to the surface.

PLAY

Vic wasn't afraid of them and calmly turned on his music. He drank his Seattle Dog while creating walls between him and the amber flock trying to kill him. Even with this outburst, Vic acknowledged they had to be helped. But from the surface world. Or so he thought. It still wasn't clear if he was led on by the clone or the mysterious God known only as GRTB. Maybe neither. What was certain is that his body started to feel the sickness that was going on all around. Given their numbers and knowing he couldn't hurt them, the alien started running. It was right there when the alien realized what a terrible world they lived in. Full of sickness and poisoned minds. Maybe his only escape was to disconnect himself from it entirely. Strangely, Alice sided with him and lured him out of there. Vic opened a hole in the wall and closed it behind him. But none of them expected what they saw on the other side.

END SIDE 1. TAPE SWITCH. SIDE 2.
PLAY

ROOSTER

And there they were... zombies. An entire army. Literally, since they were all dressed like soldiers. War veterans in fatigues. All of them were armed aside from wanting their blood. And it's when it all started. The shooting... the bombs. With no coordination whatsoever. There were less torches in this section. Mostly darkness mixed with explosive lights. Consecutive detonations of pure chaos. Vic's chest was bubbling hot behind a big rock where he took shelter with the chained underground princess. All this experience was too much for him. Not only emotional distress, but also physical weakness. He just didn't have it in him. It was affecting him somehow. All of it. And war was the culmination of all his suffering. Like a cocky rooster wanting to sing after the first rays of light only to find himself hunted by predators who destroyed all his pride. There was no more sunlight to sing to. No more faith. No more hope.

Alice started to cry. This only increased his irritability. The need to lash out at her. As if the turmoil around him made him want to displace his anger towards the people that mattered. He resented his father for making him carry this burden. A superhero's life. His thoughts were mostly on wanting to die back on Earth with the rest of humanity. But seeing Alice all broken up, gave him strength. The Will to go on. He remembered it wasn't about him. His purpose had to do with everybody else. Even damaged by all his wars, peace would come from his actions. And in that precise moment, it was Alice. Giving up on her was not an option.

Vic summoned all his courage and decided to go on the offensive. But using his head. For starters, all the guns were made from carbon steel, stainless steel and other alloys. It was similar with the bullets and the rest of their arsenal. Which meant his Earth powers could reconfigure them into something harmless. Such as gravel which he did ending the war in an instant. This didn't stop the zombies who started running towards them the moment they lost their weapons. Vic spawned a Viet Nam jungle from the ground to slow them down. The cave had stalactites that were used to take them out one by one. Stealth mode. Since the alien could also control the direction of the stalactites, there was no need for the zombies to be underneath. The rest were taken out swiftly. Using the same tactics employed to make weapons of his own. Silent weaponry such as knives, crowbars, machetes and bats. Alice followed him and helped kill half of the zombies in a similar manner. Eventually they got to all of them and could escape through a new hole Vic opened in the outer wall.

But moments before crossing, another monster came racing towards them. It kind of looked human but ran on all fours like a hell hound. A whole pack of them where regrouping in the back. He prudently decided to avoid them by closing the wall behind them. Vic turned to Alice without stopping his music and said rhetorically:

— I swear we're getting us the fuck out of here.

JUNKHEAD

In the next room, they ran across something peculiar. Crossroads leading to three doors in different colors. Each one with a torch and labeled with a specific period of the day. From left to right, the inscriptions read: Daytime (gold), Evening (brown) and Night (black). They decided to go in the suggested time order and walked towards the golden door. It was locked and was somehow immune to his transfiguration powers. As if it was made of something without matter. Even with such a warning, he still made a key from a rock and went in with Alice following closely behind. Inside they came across a strange creature in a room with many torches. It was an inverted Centaur. What appeared to be a Minotaur, but with the head of a horse instead of a bull. Vic was in defense mode but the creature approached him peacefully. Even though the monster had a mad look in his eye and seemed disoriented.

STOP

— Hey, man! — said the Horseman —. Wanna have a good time?

— Not sure on how to answer that — Vic said untrustworthily.

— Relax. I mean you no harm. I am the Hipposanthropus. But you can call me Doctor Equine.

— Do I have to?

— I insist.

— Okay, doc. So, what's the deal? Are you a real doctor or do you just play one in Greek Mythology?

— That's funny! I like that! And to answer your question, I'm not really a doctor. But I can give you the best medicine you ever had!

— Sorry, I have trust issues. Won't take anything you give me.

— You don't get it. The medicine is a game. All you have to do is chase the dragon.

— And when I catch it? What then?

— You won't be able to catch it.

— Let's say I do.

— You never will.

— So why chase it?

— Because it's fun! You'll see once you start.

— I'm not going to chase a fucking dragon! I have more important things to do.

— C'mon! Just do it once and see what happens.

— You should give it a try — Alice insisted —. Sometimes it's important to take a break from the world.

— Fine — Vic said after scoffing—. Where's the dragon?

— On the ceiling! — Doctor Equine remarked pointing upwards.

PLAY

Vic looked up and saw a very small golden dragon perched on the roof. The creature was kind of cuddly and appeared to be harmless. It had the energy of a puppy and started to move playfully at high speed. Vic started to run after it. With his Earth powers, he could easily walk on walls and the ceiling as if it was the ground itself. But the dragon was unbelievably fast. The alien even tried blocking his path with rocks and walls but the reptile was one step ahead of him every time.

Under normal circumstances, this situation would frustrate him. Irritate him. Even make his chest boil with madness. But it was the complete opposite. He felt good. Extremely good. As if he hadn't had any fun in a very long time. Alice looked happy to see him so fulfilled. She laughed so hard, it ended in violent coughing. In the end, Vic never caught the dragon as Doctor Equine assured him. But he definitely wanted to come back for more. Do it a lot. Melt his worries away. Choosing not to choose. Not caring about what everybody else thought. Thus far, by entering the realm of pleasure, his pain would be crowned king. He told Alice they had to leave that place.

DIRT

As they said their farewells from the Horseman and the dragon, Vic and Alice continued to the brown door. The same thing happened after trying to open it or morph its appearance. It was harder for him this time. As if the door was even more nihilistic than the previous one. He fashioned a new key out of a different rock and went inside. Strangely, the room was completely empty. Only a couple of torches, cave walls and sand. As he turned off his music to get a clearer perspective, Alice had a sudden mood swing that startled him deeply.

STOP

— YOU INSENSITIVE PRICK! — Alice screamed with rage.

— Sorry? — Vic asked flabbergasted.

— Why is this cave so dirty? Did you clean it? Do you care?

— What's wrong with you?

— Oh! So now there's something wrong with me because I want to live in a clean environment?

— Calm down.

— DON'T TELL ME TO CALM DOWN! It's always the same thing with you! I have to repeat myself time and time again. Everything you do is a mistake.

— Like what?

— You make me pay rent! I shouldn't have to pay for anything! You're the man! You should tend to my needs! None of my former boyfriends made me pay rent!

— Boyfriend? Are we dating?

— Lately, it doesn't seem like it. You never want to do anything with me! You only go out with your friends and leave me out of your travels.

— I really don't know what you're talking about.

— Obviously, you don't! You never make love to me. You fall asleep, snore and make me want to sleep in different rooms all the time. Do you want me to take a lover as well? You don't think I had opportunities on the street? Surely anybody would be much better than you in every single way.

— Hey, you're starting to piss me off.

— Am I? I don't care! Ever wonder why we never have kids? Because I don't want to bring a child into this world that is just as fucked up as you are. You'll never receive my compassion for being Bipolar. Your tears are meaningless, so don't you ever cry in front of me. You're not special for being "sick" nor does it give you talents of any kind. All your virtues come from your shirt which is probably dirty and full of holes. I work sixteen hours straight and you stay home in bed all day. Have you no ambition like me? Do you want to be the mediocre fuck that you have been your whole life? You really should die and leave this world. It would be so much better without you in it. And don't worry. I'll send a message to your family so I'm not legally responsible for your suicide.

— ENOUGH!

PLAY

The alien summoned quicksand below Alice's feet. She started to cry while sinking slowly. Very slowly. Vic's chest was about to explode with radiation. Grunge music was needed badly. So, he sat on the ground and focused on the words that would bring him peace. He couldn't help but glance at Alice every now and then. The words she mouthed were clear to him. "I'm sorry", "Let's try again", "I love you" ... but there was no solution to her toxic nature. An exit strategy was required immediately. Maybe return to the first room. But there was no going back. The feeling of loss was imminent. And he was losing her too. Little by little.

What happened? How did they end up like this? None of it made any sense. It was like going from Heaven to Hell in an instant. Like living in a long-term relationship without remembering anything. Did it actually happen? Had so much time passed by without even realizing it? Or was it all a hoax? And if it was, who was responsible for it? The clone, the Church of H, the food, the God of Letters, the zombies, the strange humanoids, Doctor Equine, the dragon, Alice... all of them? There was only one way to know for sure. By saving her. Even if it wasn't a trick, Vic really did care about Alice and couldn't watch her die. But, for some strange reason, there was no stopping the quicksand...

Vic got up and extended his arm. She reached out from the marsh and grabbed his hand. In that exact moment, they switched positions. Now Vic was drowning in the quicksand and Alice was pulling him out. He was able to exit with her help while slowly regaining his superpowers to stop the moving dirt entirely.

STOP

— What the fuck just happened? — Vic asked confused.

— I don't know — Alice said equally troubled —. You went into a weird trance once we entered the room. Then you summoned the quicksand and jumped in.

— Wait... you don't remember our conversation?

— Vic, we never spoke in this room. You just threw yourself into the dirt. As if you wanted to be swallowed whole.

— We have to leave this place. NOW!

— Are you sure you don't want to go into the first room again? You looked happy.

— It's too late for that. We have to move on to the third door.

Alice and Vic left the room. In the end, he got the answer he was looking for. The person responsible for all of it... was himself.

PLAY

GOD SMACK

As they walked out the door, Alice began to feel extremely sick. Her face was pale and she started throwing up. Somehow Vic thought that if they completed the cycle and went through the black door, all their suffering would come to an end. He was about to find out how wrong he was.

The alien crafted a new key to enter the last and final door with the word "Night" etched over the dark surface. On the other end, there were many charts of the humanoids he saw earlier. Apparently, it was medical related data. The words "clone", "Tissue sample" and "No bone" came up in all of them. There were also many sophisticated machines with electrical lights and a strange altar with countless unlit candles, a painting of the Last Supper and a puppy in a jar of flies. Mister H was there waiting for him.

STOP

— I'm surprised you made it this far — Mister H said smiling diabolically—. Though, I was counting on it.

— YOU! — Vic cried out in anger —. You were the one behind this the whole time! I knew I couldn't trust a clone!

— And yet you did. You don't know why and it's eating you up inside, isn't it?

— I wanted to leave since I got here. I never bought into this cult madness.

— But you never left either. You could have opened the Earth above you at any time. Go to the surface and pull yourself out. But instead, you kept going down through my maze of doors. Fucking yourself up in the pre-funk to meet me exactly where I wanted you to.

— You used some sort of mental manipulation like Black Silence. That's how you duped the Yellow People into believing you were their Savior.

— Mental manipulation? Hardly. It's really much simpler than that. You see, I also have a superpower.

— Sucking your own dick in the name of the Lord is not a superpower.

— You must have me confused with somebody who gives a fuck about religion.

— Don't bullshit me. You have a monk haircut under that cap, don't you?

— Please. I'm so much more! When I first got here, the Yellow People didn't trust me because of my human appearance. So, I was confined in four walls as far as I could remember. Fuckers left me there to die! A prison that, however, was under a poppy field. My only source of nourishment for eons. What would have killed a normal human, had its advantages for a clone engineered for immortality. The power to absorb narcotic properties and infect their sedative nature to those around me. Delivered in small doses but calibrated at will.

— Hold on... you mean you're the man in the box buried in your shit?

— More like an animal before the slaughter. But I got the last laugh. With my powers, I could trick them into believing. A very simple Heaven and Hell scenario. Give them my golden touch packed with hope for God and making them fear the torment of becoming zombies. Of course, they would all become zombies eventually. After a while, I needed to drain souls to enhance my powers. Hence, the living dead. Since all their urges were reduced to the drug itself, I could control them even easier after killing them. But while their needs became greater, as did mine. It pissed me off at first that I couldn't make them pass out or overdose. Until I realized it was a far better solution. Because the real craft was to drain them gradually. Unnoticed to the naked eye. Mistaking my false happiness for their own when in truth all they were feeling was pure opiate dependance. As you personally have experienced yourself.

— So, smack is the God. Mister H... Heroin...

— Bingo.

— Then all that door crap I went through never happened?

— What do you want to hear? That you went to a magical place or that you laid comatose with a needle in your arm throughout your whole quest? Fact is, I still needed you for the final part of my plan. The god was spoken in specific words that I needed as a code to spawn my creature of destruction. One that would make me all powerful and turn everybody into zombies under my control.

— Wasn't cloning four-legged mutants enough for you?

— Oh... that comes later...

— You mean after you sacrifice them in your pagan altar?

— A failed experiment, I'm afraid. I tried to summon an ancient Jewish Golem that never came to be. My 2.0 version was backed by advanced tech given to me by your former foe, Black Silence.

— So GRTB is just a code?

— Two of the worst serial killers to ever set foot in the state of Washington.

— Gary Ridgeway and Ted Bundy.

— Very good. With their combined aura, I now can summon... well, as you nicely put it, the GOD SMACK! The ugliest and most gruesome monster ever seen!

— You're gonna make it look like yourself?

— FUCK YOU!

— You know what I just realized? All supervillains are very dumb. They always reveal their plans and weaknesses. Only Ozymandias got it right.

— But you're not going to hurt me, are you? I'm pretty sure you want me in your life forever. Do you want me to die?

— No... I don't.

— You're still thinking about the golden door, aren't you?

— Yes...

— And you're going to sit back and let me drain everyone on the planet with my God Smack?

— That's where you're wrong. Alice and I will stop you.

— Alice? Oh, you naive fuck! You do know she's not real?

— What? — Vic said knowing already in his gut what he was about to say.

— Well— Mister H continued —, sort of real. If you're religious like those fools in the Yellow City. Alice is your soul. Your life force. I simply detached the vision of yourself through Deaf Metal tech. Your father's cloning technology had a spiritual perk as it also displaced matter from energy. Illusion from Reality. It's how I drain lives. It turns out you began to lose your precious Alice since you got here. It's very easy to brainwash a forgotten soul and warp a soulless mind towards deception. Why do you think she was so respectful of my persona since the beginning? Forgetting all about her connection to you? You didn't follow her in here. You were hooked on me since I cleaned your wound. Losing yourself in my narcotic fueled delusions thinking all the while you were helping her. But it was the exact opposite of that. I had to break your spirit in order to move forward. And now she's on the verge of dying. Which brings me to the final part of my plan and why I needed you in the first place.

As Vic turned to Alice, she was lying very weak on the ground. Mister H spoke both serial killer names on an intercom on the wall. This activated the machines and drained her into oblivion. Before disappearing, Alice looked at the alien and said her own combination of letters: MSSK. The ground started to shake. And it wasn't his powers. But the creature in the clone's prophecy. The presence levitated the supervillain and swirled around him until a behemoth-like creature was formed as an armor with Mister H at its heart. The golden-brown elephant humanoid broke from his subterranean lair, crushing the ground above him. His tusks resembled that of a mammoth and his eyes where glowing vermilion red. The monster was twenty stories high and his elongated trunk would serve the purpose of draining the life force of all the Window World inhabitants. Fueled by a twin serial killer aura and a Psychotic Dealer. Behold the God Smack!

Vic stood by and watched all of it happen. Just like the supervillain said he would. His addiction was beyond redemption and any life without the drug that flooded his veins was inconceivable. His withdrawal symptoms started to peak. He went to a nearby cavern to evacuate all his fluids. All which left him empty. The literal equivalent of not having a soul. Like a demon clinging to

Hell for comfort. The alien didn't even turn on his music because he knew it wouldn't help him. Until he remembered Alice's dying words.

Surely the letters were names, as was the case with the serial killers. References that were known to him since Alice was a part of himself. Thinking about his music again, the epiphany revealed itself as Mike Starr and Sean Kinney. Fact is, Earth is the bass and drums of Creation. And like the God Smack, the words needed to be spoken to the first failed Golem to revive him. Though not Jewish himself, Vic remembered a philology class he took and his rudimentary knowledge of the ancient languages like Latin, Greek and, for his current predicament, Hebrew. After a while of remembering, he uttered the AIC member names to invoke the Golem:

— מייק סטאר ושון קיני

The puppy in the jar came alive suddenly and crawled out of the jar of flies. It aged until an adult size instantly but had only three legs. The tripod dog then proceeded to bark at the Last Supper portrait. Jesus and the Apostles came to life in the painting and raised their hands at the same time. Divine fire lit the thirteen candles which in turn summoned a great ball of dirt that grew and grew with the heat. It eventually transformed into a giant Golem. Though it didn't look like the traditional Jewish creature. It looked more like Bobo, the Gorilla. Basically, because the terraformed ape skull happened to be buried where the magical configuration took place. Using the creature's muddy skin to hover, the superhero advanced up to the creature's shoulder.

PLAY

Vic controlled the Dirt Golem as if it was his own body. Maybe there was no way to hurt the supervillain directly, but it could be done through a Jewish protector. There was a clear disadvantage since the clone had the God Smack worn as an armor whereas the alien was exposed in the openair. On the other hand, that gave him a better advantage sense-wise. When he located the creature, it was already drawing energy from the planet itself with its trunk. It wouldn't take long for Mister H to drain all the Crystal People in Window World. Vic got the monster's attention by throwing a huge rock against its back. The great beast stopped and turned around with rage. The Dirt Golem ran towards its foe and started hitting the hellephant with everything it had. The

God Smack fought back with equal force and the battle went on for a while. But the Golem was fueled with the alien's wrath. The best defense is a strong offense, as they say. And his punches were not only powerful, but really fast. Having the God Smack at his mercy, the Dirt Golem delivered his final blow with Vic shouting:

— FUCKING NAZIS DIE!!!

IRON GLAND

The God Smack started to disintegrate slowly until fully collapsing to the ground. It exploded rendering the Dirt Golem inactive with the expanding wave of serial killer energy. Vic no longer had control over the colossus.

HATE TO FEEL

M ister H was on the floor. He lost his cap and had many cuts and bruises. But having the powers he had, the supervillain never actually felt pain. Which explained his sociopathic behavior. Though still addicted, Vic approached him willing to fight.

STOP

— For the record — Mister H said getting up —, I'm not a Nazi like your former squeeze toy.

— I know — Vic confirmed —, but I was atop a divine Jewish creation. Seemed like the appropriate thing to say.

— How's that working out for you, by the way?

— My Ex? Love, Hate, Love... give or take.

— That makes it easier on me. Lost love always leads to self-destruction. And that's my turf. You remind me of your old man. The junkie part at least.

— My dad was a junkie?

— Who do you think gave the order to plant the first poppy fields in Pill Hill?

— And me thinking he was overly fond of poppy seed bagels.

— Crack all the jokes you want. But you know deep down you can't beat me. I might have lost the God Smack, but I'm still the God of Smack.

— Are you sure you're not the Shit God? I always have the runs after talking to you.

— Why do you think that is? You're dependent on me. You won't turn zombie because of your flannel, but you're still at my mercy every inch of the way.

— News flash, asshole. Heroes are forged in sacrifice. And by sacrificing my craving and addictions, I can kick the living shit out of you if need be. Besides, I'm Bipolar. I'm used to going opposite of my suicidal nature.

— Really? You don't want me around anymore? Take the pain away in a haze of pleasure? Help you die even? Your withdrawal symptoms are fading just by being close to me.

— It's only sustenance now. I get no joy out of it. As much as I hate to feel reality, I hate you fucking clones even more.

— Okay... let's say you decide to summon the rehab in you to stay away. What about my army?

— What army?

— Don't think I'm just a Monster Necromancer. I control the dead themselves. While I escape with oceans of my zombie minions in between, think about why you're chasing me. Is it because you want to stop me or stop your suffering with another hit?

— My suffering will stop when I beat you.

— Yeah, good luck with that.

Mister H smiled and raised his glowing fist into the air. All the zombies above came running and crowded around him like loyal dogs. Among the zombies there, a living dead crystal horse showed up which the villain mounted immediately. The clone rode off leaving him with all the undead Crystal People to deal with. The addiction, the withdrawal, the lost energy on the Golem and the absence of a soul had left the alien in a fragile state. Without enough Will to keep the supervillain from escaping. But enough to summon a small terrain to escape himself a few miles away. Vic ended up crashing in the Lumen Field football stadium where he rested for a while knowing well all the zombies would find him sooner or later.

PLAY

The Grunge Rock Alien sat down in the End Zone and closed his eyes as if meditating. Trying to harness the energy beneath him. Every mineral, every element... the Earth itself. If he had descended into Hell, there had to be a Heaven beside him. His chest was bubbling with Bipolar insanity mixed with the need to satisfy his demonic urges. But soon music and nature came through, calming his radioactive side to focus on what was important. The born-again superhero started to hover slightly with grains of dirt surrounding him like planets. He opened his glowing amber eyes to see a large group of zombies running towards him on the other end of the field. Vic stood on his feet and walked a few steps where he found a jersey of the running back, Marshawn Lynch.

Though not familiar with sports out of the 90s, the alien still put on the football jersey and forged a dirt football to cling too. This had no specific purpose other than to thrill himself. The only good thing about chasing the dragon was the ability to take time and enjoy life's little pleasures. Though this got him hooked immediately, the lesson was the same. The purpose of life was the journey and the meaning was leaving one's mark. In this case literally, since he was avoiding zombies, breaking tackles and stiff arming the whole lot while creating a beast quake scoring the touchdown. The Richter scale effect was so great, that it cracked the earth outside the stadium where he exited. Most zombies trying to get in fell into the fault. Vic kept his momentum and jumped high in the air performing an all-out Stage Dive which in turn created a seismic wave in the living dead mosh pit. The resulting effect shattered all the undead in a single aftershock.

ANGRY CHAIR

Vic felt remorse for killing all those zombies. But it was clear that, even if a cure was found, they were too far gone on the mortal plane. As the alien understood from his personal struggle with addiction. He wanted to kick his habit indefinitely. Not only because of his own health, but because Mister H could only be beaten by being sober. And there was only one way to do that.

To kill two birds with one stone, ending both his remorse for killing and his dependance, Vic took off the football jersey and reconfigured most of the zombies with his Earth powers. This is the reason why he didn't turn into a zombie himself. Glass was in the most part sand silicates and some limestone. So, the new-found Light Necromancer could revive the dead to fit his needs. In this case, resuscitating them as recovering addicts. They were no longer zombies, but were just as addicted to Mister H's influence as he was. They congregated in an abandoned building that fortuitously had many chairs which all of them contributed to arrange in a large circle. They needed each other. The group, the higher power and all the philosophy behind rehab.

STOP

Vic heard their testimonies. Every one of them. Pouring out the soul he personally had lost. Directed towards religion, faith and God. Some of them becoming born again worshipers. Exactly like the Yellow People underground. But believing in a true benign power. The alien wasn't religious at all. Nor could he relate to the addicts that weren't. And what was supposed to help him, was actually making him angry. Irritating him as never before. Sitting there. Craving another hit and the sad thought of never doing it again. The Hell of withdrawal burning him inside. In that chair. Apathetic. Helpless. Alone. The alien wasn't buying into all the spiritual side of it. How could he? Alice was no longer with him. The cloud everybody was praying to was completely gray to him. There was no way to imagine tranquility up to this point. Until one of the addicts enumerated the steps towards recovery.

Vic didn't focus that much on what was really being suggested, as for the allegory behind it. The steps had a clear theme: Humility. Accepting you have no control, the higher power, forgiveness, inventory... everything... was just a means to be humble. Which meant addiction was really all Pride. That was the real reason for his anger and not believing in general. Deep down the superhero thought himself a god. Somebody who could control and do everything he wanted. Vic thought back to the bone epiphany acquired before entering the Yellow City. The answer was in front of him the whole time. So, with this in mind and after everybody's testimony, the alien articulated a dissertation of his own:

— Hi, I'm Vic and I'm an addict.

— HI VIC!!!! — the rest of the group said ecstatic.

— Up until now, I never realized the problem. I'm not special. I'm an alien with powers, a human, a Messiah, a savior, a superhero, a god... bullshit. I'm no different than any other living being. I know that now. I can't control everything and there are forces... higher powers... that far exceed my capabilities. My addiction is my fault. Self-chosen pain. It was my decision. Something I won't be able to control ever. Nobody can. I always thought Reason could control Passion. Like driving a car. And since I started, I thought I was basically another drunk driver trying to steer into the clear. But now I know the car was speeding but nobody was at the wheel. The doors to my doom were locked, but I still made the keys to go in. And to recover, I need to close the door behind me and lock myself out. Thanks a lot for the wake-up call. Listening to your testimonies made me see that I'm not alone. That I can do this. With help. And not by myself. Because being on your own, trying to control something more powerful and keep killing yourself thinking you're invulnerable is just plain arrogant. And I'm not arrogant. Not anymore. I'm truly sorry I hurt you all. I hope you can forgive me. But most importantly, I hope I can forgive myself...

A great silence spread across the room for a minute. A very long minute. Until they all started to clap. One after the other. Culminating in a general cheer. Vic felt much better. Especially after hearing a familiar voice from within.

— Vic? — Alice said in voice over mode.

— Alice? — Vic said questioning his own Being—. You're alive!

— I'm immortal, silly. I never disappeared. You only got lost within yourself. And you succeeded where many have failed. Humility is the hidden power you needed to unlock to have my undying protection. You may now confront that piece of shit again. I got your back.

— You got it, Soul Sister!

— Soul Sister?

— Sorry. Sounded funnier in my head.

— We are in your head.

— Never mind.

Alice laughed with a sweet voice timber that filled his heart. And sweetness was something he rarely had contact with. Shortly after, her aura covered him in gold. It was the glowing manifestation of Will.

PLAY

Vic said his goodbyes to the group and fused into the ground. Henceforth proceeding to dig at incredible speed with a Big-Bertha-like drill coming from his fists. The superhero advanced through all types of soils and metals in the ground as well as artefacts and fossils from former civilizations and ecosystems. Even some sort of life on the other side... Though it was very different from his planet, there was a strong connection there. As if his existence was a small part of a bigger picture. Humility not only unlocked his soul but the wisdom to see the universe as it really was: chaos connected by the entropy of life. And in the spirit of being humble and in line of what was said in the group, there was no way to beat the clone by himself. And lacking friends in this zone, Vic had to ask the most unlikely of creatures for help.

WOULD?

Vic could send telepathic messages through plant roots as if they were electric cables. He could also track any ground signature above him. There wasn't going to be many horses in the Yellow City. So, it all came down to the horseshoe pattern on the dirt. It didn't take him long to locate the supervillain and pinpoint his position. Vic thrusted from the soil with a powerful punch, throwing Mister H off his horse. The superhero landed in front of him without the fear that plagued him to become addicted again. Alice was his real rehab. And she kept her promise. He could feel her. The craving didn't go away, but his Will kept him at bay. Being immune to the supervillain's narcotic charm.

STOP

— You never learn, do you? — Mister H said smiling and calmly getting up.

— Actually — Vic said hitting him twice with fists made of diamonds and knocking him to the ground —, I do.

— But? How... THAT'S IMPOSSIBLE!

— Nope. That's the force of humility, cocksucker. You have no effect on me anymore.

— Is that so? — Mister H said getting up again with a yellow sphere in his hand —. DOOM ORB... PLAY COUNTRY MUSIC!

— Fuck my Sludge Factory. Forgot about that.

An extremely Country version of the "Midnight Special" song started playing. Vic fell to his knees in agony.

— It's only Country music — Vic said trying to convince himself —. It's not that bad...

— Then why are you so weak? — Mister H said smiling.

— Can you at least play the Creedence version?

— Do you think I'm an idiot?

— Uh... yeah.

— Creedence Clear Water Revival would only make you stronger!

— Well, it was worth the shot.

— Now I will displace your soul once again to have you at my mercy.

— I wouldn't do that if I were you.

— Really? Why is that?

— Let's just say you underestimate Alice. She's much more powerful than you realize.

— Even if that were true, she harnesses said power from you. And now I have you pussy-whipped.

— That's why I didn't come alone. STAR DOG... A LITTLE HELP HERE!

The Sentinel appeared atop a nearby hill armed with a crossbow made of bones. Lucky for the alien, the city's protector was inside the Yellow City at the time and could hear his cries for help. Star Dog shot an arrow with precision, destroying the Doom Orb in the villain's hand. The dog fled shortly after shouting:

— WOOD COULD, MADERFAKAAAAAAA!

PLAY

Vic got up with a gonna-kick-your-ass-now sneer on his face. Deaf to the alien's warning, Mister H believed his soul could be detached and broken as before. He used the Displacement Tech on him to extract his spirit once more. Alice appeared floating above and covered in chains. But to his surprise, she broke all of them in a show of super-strength that already gave him a hint of what was expected. Before even thinking about the beating he was about to receive, Alice disappeared and reappeared from different angles with kicks and punches of all styles. The momentum started to speed up until she knocked Mister H out entirely. As a final display of his powers, Vic reconstructed Seattle from scratch, rearranging every molecule to create buildings, houses and businesses in general.

TAPE STOPPED

NOW THE YELLOW CITY was brand new. All the citizens settled underground joyfully ascended to the streets using staircases created by the alien. They were cured of the zombie virus now that Mister H had been beaten. In the surface they were informed by the recovering addicts about the false prophet and founded a New Republic. Vic watched from a distance while taking his yellow flannel shirt off.

— Told you this would happen, dickhead — the alien said while securing the shirt around the villain's waist to imprison him in dirt chains.

— I'm proud of you, Vic — Alice said smiling.

— I must give you most of the credit on this one, sweetheart.

— You never learn, do you?

— Why does everybody keep saying that?

— It was a team effort. Everyone did their part. And you played an important role in all of this. You know, there's such a thing as being too humble.

— Yeah, it's called depression.

— Good one — Alice replied giggling.

— Well, anyone who can make his soul laugh is already immortal.

— Don't drift too much towards the other end.

— No worries — Vic said merrily —. I have you to keep me in check. We're permanently displaced now, aren't we?

— I'm afraid not. I will always be with you. But your fight is always your own.

— How are we going to merge then?

— Eyes are the windows of the soul.

— What?

Instead of explaining it, Alice directly got in through Vic's eyes in an ectoplasmic tornado.

— That was unsettling — Vic said stunned.

Soon after, the Alternative Valkyrie hologram appeared before him. The statue still had his mother's face with a few alterations in her clothing. Vic kneeled and expressed his depravities:

— Bless me Goddess, for I have sinned. I sought to cry out "God is Dead!" to the cult leader while drinking a bucket of hot dogs.

At times wanted to fuck my own soul. Spike my football to the planet's core hoping it would explode. Keep the dragon as a pet and name him after the Simpsons band, Sadgasm. Become a zombie to appreciate the goddamn Seattle rain water. Use the Dirt Golem to kill whoever made the Country Midnight Special version and felt like hitting everybody in rehab with a chair.

As always, a piece of paper fell from the sky. This time, the word "Sparks" was written on it. He fainted shortly after.

PART FOUR: NIRVANA

Vic woke up in his ship once again. He had triumphed over evil on three counts and had one more city left to go. The idea that it was all a dream still overwhelmed him. Maybe this was already death and life was the dream. Either way, ending his quest was the only way to unveil the whole plot. The Grunge Rock Alien's last journey into the unknown. The superhero looked down at the final tape he would hear. One labelled *NEVERMIND* by the band Nirvana. The image in the cover was very curious. A baby chasing a dollar bill on a hook underwater. Perhaps a symbol that we are all born into consumerism and that the System will lure you into their ideals and customs from the start. Thus, shunning those who don't take the bait. While pondering about this, he went to the closet where the final flannel shirt was waiting for him with its dark scarlet color. The alien put it on and marched out of his spaceship towards the Red Zone.

PLAY

SMELLS LIKE TEEN SPIRIT

For some strange reason, everything turned to slow motion by going east. Not only that, the road was not deserted like the previous ones. There were many human highschoolers on both sides of the moon-like surface which included cheerleaders, jocks, nerds, rich kids, poor kids, popular kids, slackers, rebels, band members, loners, misfits, hipsters, skaters, Christians, hippies and a janitor. Though the music was inspiring enough to calm his radioactive chest pains, the large crowd started to annoy him. As did the strong scent of deodorant. His face expression was of pure anger. Vic was always watchful seeing that most of them had guns and cocked them as he passed by. There were also two out of place characters with strange weapons. A werewolf with a shiny gun and a nun with a furry revolver.

Everything looked like false information. The same principle that was seen in the Nevermind cover. As if entertainment was created to blind our eyes from the truth. But what wasn't there? Some of the people where in groups as if part of the same System. But the few that weren't, were outcasts in their own personal worlds. This made him feel like more of an outcast. Trying to fit in easily with his own was more difficult than with extraterrestrial life. Even with the potential of fame and greatness. As with humility before, Vic was worse at what he was good at. Fame made him infamous and the struggle to belong transformed him into something he wasn't. The idea that the strange people were clones themselves came to mind, but it was easier to pretend they weren't even there.

Reaching the end of the road, the entrance to the Red City was ornamented with a Temple facade. The last Sentinel stood by its gates. An astronaut made of stone who was dancing and squirming like a snake. Vic approached the dancing pilot and asked him the most obvious question that popped into his head.

STOP

— So — Vic said sticking out his hand with a muddled look on his face —, what the fuck just happened back there?

— Hey GRA! — the Astronaut said showing off his dance moves—. Welcome to the Red!

— What do I call you? Rock Astronaut?

— Actually, it's Stone Pilot.

— The East Road Sentinel?

— I AM, I AM, I AM...

— Stop. I believe you. Can you answer my question now? I'm crazy and a recovering addict so I don't know what's real anymore.

— Well, it's a difficult question to answer. They were real and they weren't.

— How is that even possible?

— What is the illusion? Isn't reality an illusion of what's real in our minds? Do we see reality as it is or are our illusions the mainframe of everything that's real?

— Please don't tell me that was the riddle.

— No, the riddle will come from the visual display you have seen and a two-part puzzle you need to answer.

— Oh, that's fucking great! I must answer two riddles then? It's always the same story with these... COULD YOU PLEASE STOP DANCING!!!

— Okay, okay — the Stone Pilot replied standing still—. What a party pooper. Highschoolers, you may now fade into nothingness.

— Hang on... you created them?

— Why do you think I was dancing? Look behind you. They're gone. My personal delusions, Bruh.

— Fuck me — Vic said turning his head to a deserted road and back to the Sentinel—. The smell of deodorant was you as well?

— That I don't know. I'm usually smelling like a rose.

— Why are you made of stone then?

— Space Medusa.

— Oh, please. There's no such thing!

— Fine, I got wasted and woke up this way. Happy?

— So, you're like half a man in there?

— Not like I used to be.

— You're the only Sentinel with superpowers?

— We all have powers. I'm just not afraid to show them off.

— How modest of you.

— How modest of them, you mean.

— Yeah, I was being sarcastic.

— For what purpose?

— Never mind. Can you please tell me the hyper-combo riddle now?

— Right. First part. What smell did the smell of deodorant smell like?

— I asked you the same thing earlier!

— And I didn't answer you because you had to answer, crackerman.

— Fine, let me think about it for a moment... since all of them were teens like me, I imagine it has to do with Teen Spirit. But as it was an illusion, I'm going to say just Teens.

— Wow! Not bad. You're not at all stupid as we Sentinels originally thought!

— WHAT?!

— Let's move on. The Superman can only kill with one gun as only one gun can kill the Superman. Where in the crowd can he kill or be killed?

— Technically, that's three riddles.

— I said two-part. Not two.

— Whatever... the werewolf. He had a silver gun which the Superman would use to kill him or make him kill himself seeing how the monster would be immune to any other attack. I can't believe I just said that.

— But it's correct! And the second gun?

— The fuzzy one. The nun with the velvet revolver.

— Why?

— Because, being a Superman, he would be prepared for any type of gun. Except something innocent he would never see coming. Like being shot by a nun with a revolver that looks like a stuffed animal.

— Great! You did it! You may pass now. Hope you have a good time in there.

— I doubt it. Everybody's an asshole. Specially the clones.

— You mean President Woke?

— I guess.

— Yep. An evil asshole. I only like Mister H.

— Well, don't. Trust me. He's one of the worst ones.

— But you'll have a good time.

— How do you know?

— Because I can FEEEEEL iiiiiiIIIIT!

— Of course you can. Nice meeting you, Stone Pilot. Oh, you can keep dancing now.

— You don't have to tell me twice!

PLAY

IN BLOOM

Vic entered the Red City which was equally constructed as the Purple City. In other words, not too high tech as the Blue City or as devastated as the Yellow City. His red flannel began to shine like sparklers. Apparently, the elemental power in this zone was Fire. This confused him for a bit. As it was with the former cover, the correlation was exact. Earth for Dirt. But now it was Fire for Water. Though the first two albums had little to do with the element in question. So maybe it was nothing. Or was it?

Vic noticed his flying powers returned. But they were slightly different from the others. Flames burst out from the bottom of his feet making him hover and fly at incredible speed. The alien experimented for a while; twirling in the air and leaving a streak of smoke in his tracks. The Seattle rain had no effect in putting him out, but a sudden shotgun explosion awakened his superhero sense.

A Redneck Crystal Posse (that was their actual name) was using a clay pigeon launcher to fling targets into the sky. But these targets weren't discs. They were bullying a Red Crystal thirteen-year-old nerd and blowing up all his possessions to smithereens. Since Vic hated that ultra-macho-be-a-man stereotype, he decided to go down and help. When the Rednecks flung the teen's backpack, he intercepted it and landed in front of them. As the teenager was given his backpack, Vic signaled him to stand behind him. The expected hostility from the Posse was surprisingly the opposite when the jock-like redneck with the shotgun spoke to him in admiration.

STOP

— Hey! — the redneck cried out —. You're that alien young'un who's into them rock music tapes.

— Hmm, yeah — Vic replied confused —. What about them?

— Name's Brody. I love me some rock music too! Reckon we should listen to granny-slapping tunes together. Maybe grab a rack over yonder to pass the time.

— Sorry, Brody. Not interested. Something about everything you said doesn't seem right. You know the meaning behind rock songs?

— Darn-tooting.'

— I doubt that.

— Right ornery of ya. Think yer shit don't stink!

— Okay, let's put it to the test. If I name any Queen song, can you explain what it means?

— Don't listen to them fudgepacker albums. Can't carry a tune in a bucket and useless as tits on a bull.

— Okay... I'll kick the shit out of you later for that remark. But now let's go with something heavier. War Pigs- Black Sabbath.

— Yeah, love me some Sabbath. Song's about the Devil fucking a piranha.

— What the fuck? No! It's a song against war. Led Zeppelin – Ramble on.

— Bout' people who rough talks and gets back some sugar.

— Wrong again. It's a tribute and reference to Tolkien's Lord of the Rings depicting a way to "ramble" or wander to find true love. The Beatles- Helter Skelter.

— Fucking hippies killing a high cotton lady hotter than a goat's butt in a pepper patch. All out racial war, boy!

— Wrong and hat-trick, Brody. Helter Skelter is a British fairground attraction with a slide that McCartney uses as a symbol of the rise and fall of the Roman Empire; being ultimately the latter. What you're saying has to do with the Manson Family. That happened after and was a complete misinterpretation of the lyrics! Which is the same fucking nonsense you're doing!

— Ain't you the uppity type.

— Bet you got this whole clay pigeon idea from a song you thought was telling you to pull this crazy shit.

— Yes siree.

— Which song?

— Beatles tune too, boy. All you need is love.

— Get the fuck out of here! You're an embarrassment to Rock N' Roll!

— You dern starting to piss me off, son!

— It wasn't a request — Vic said setting the launcher ablaze with his right hand —. Fuck off!

— Fine, alien — Brody said realizing he was outgunned —. We'll skedaddle. But next time we see you, y'all won't be so lucky. LET'S GO, BOYS!

The Redneck Crystal Posse fled while whistling, yelling and shooting in the air. Some of them even gave Vic the stink eye. But there was no fear in his heart. Not even after what the boy would tell him.

— Are you okay? — Vic asked the teenager.

— No yeah — the nerd answered bashfully—. Thank you. I'm Danny.

— Nice to meet you, Danny. I'm Vic. Who were those guys?

— The Redneck Crystal Posse. Hardcore Southern Rednecks.

— Southern? Near Window World Mexico, right?

— Where else?

— Whatever. Tell me about them.

— They run half of the crimes in the city.

— And the other half?

— Rainbow Ninjas.

— What the fuck is a Rainbow Ninja?

— Well... like a normal ninja, but extraordinarily gay. They also wear those ninja pajamas in multicolor instead of black.

— Isn't the purpose of black in ninjitsu to go by unnoticed?

— You probably haven't seen the Red City. Gay Pride flags everywhere.

— President Woke?

— He's incredibly PC. Though he doesn't take sides as far as the Posse and the Ninjas are concerned.

— Are the Rainbow Ninjas as bad as the Redneck Crystal Posse?

— Same. But they're the other side of the coin. PC Fundamentalists regarding Gay Rights. They're known as Homophobe Assassins. Reason why they're at war with the Posse.

— Okay, thanks for the intel. What about you?

— What about me?

— I mean… do you know who you are and what you want to be?

— I'm not really sure. I don't even know if I like boys, girls… or either.

— Don't worry about it. It will come to you once you're in bloom. But be careful. It's becoming more and more dangerous to have an identity these days. And I don't mean the PC kind.

— I'll do that. Thanks again for saving me.

— Anytime, kid.

PLAY

Vic took off with his fire thrusting feet and waved goodbye to his nerdy outcast friend. Getting caught in the crossfire of these two extremist gangs was his main concern. Yet he never expected it to be so soon.

COME AS YOU ARE

As the alien was flying and leaving a streak of smoke in the sky, his leg was struck with a six-point shuriken. The subsequent crash occurred on the rooftop of the Morck Hotel. He removed the ninja star from his leg which left a small wound with hardly any blood. Vic examined the shuriken and noticed the edges where all cock-shaped with a hole in the middle fashioned like an anus.

STOP

— What the flying fuck is this? — Vic said baffled while getting up.

— We meet at last, hot stuff — said a ninja among another group of ninjas in multicolored shinobis.

— OMG... are you Care Bears?

— Do we look like fucking Care Bears?

— Only one way to know for sure. Show me your tummies and tell me that I matter. But really mean it.

— You done, joke boy?

— Rainbow Ninjas, I presume.

— Konnichiwa, motherfucker.

— I think that line would sound better with "Sayonara." Though it's more of a Schwarzenegger quote. You would have to be tough guys and I don't see that in ninjas crapped from a rainbow.

— Are you saying we're not tough because we're gay? You homophobic fuck!

— Not because you're gay. Because of your tacky fashion sense. And I come from the Grunge Era, asshole. We basically invented the antihomophobia movement. And being antihomophobic is very different from forced inclusion.

— In what way?

— One thing is for a heterosexual to accept somebody's sexual preferences and another to force heterosexuals to include the LGBTIQA+ community in everything. It's not about taking one picture with everyone in it. It's about a photo album of different preferences enriching humanity as a whole.

— You insensitive piece of shit! You don't know what you're talking about!

— Don't I? Do you realize that because of this PC bullshit people are acting like they're expected to act like instead of being themselves? The fear of getting attacked has turned everybody into sheep. Self-censorship at its worst. When everybody should really just come as they are.

— What if I rather cum on your face?

— If I say no, that would make me a homophobe, right?

— Obviously!

— So, I have to be gay to be considered antihomophobic? That doesn't sound right to me.

— Maybe for a homophobe who doesn't give a shit about inclusion.

— Let's say you write a play with an all-gay cast and story. Would it be fair if I told you to include heterosexual themes and people in it? LGBTIQA+ rights are not about being included in everything or to impose those beliefs on anybody who isn't. It's about letting people think and choose whatever the fuck they want without anybody telling them differently.

— You don't get it!

— More than you think, Pride Pajamas. I have the soul of a girl. Though I think she's a lesbian because I love women. Sometimes in the Closer-Nine Inch Nails type of way.

— SHUT THE FUCK UP!

— Fine, I want to fuck them like an animal all the time.

— I MEAN STOP TALKING, VARMINT!

— Varmint? You're a redneck all of the sudden? Couldn't care less. Point being, this shit isn't new. Back in my planet, I would call it Human Stupidity 101: "Think like me or I'll destroy you".

— You're right about the destruction part.

— That being the case— Vic said approaching the ninja and kissing him on the lips through his mask—, you broke my heart.

— I thought you weren't gay — the ninja said surprised.

— I'm not. It's more of an antihomophobic Godfather thing.

— What?

Vic punched the ninja with flamed knuckles and hurled him against an air conditioner vent. The martial art homosexual vanished as if by some magical art or strange power.

— OH NO YOU DIDN'T! — another ninja said in an effeminate voice after snapping his fingers.

PLAY

The Rainbow Ninjas attacked him. One by one. Punching, kicking and flipping in the air. To which the alien only took evasive action. This was going to be a difficult victory. Particularly because he had no martial art training whatsoever. Vic wanted to end it quickly but he didn't have a gun. So instead, the superhero ignited a fire aura around him. Which was really a defense mechanism against the fifty Rainbow Ninjas gathered on that rooftop. This would force the long-distance battle as to avoid getting burned with punches and kicks delivered at close range. But it was Vic's plan from the start. Though he still wondered how well it worked. As if the ninjas were afraid of Fire.

The assumption was that they would use their ninja stars or anything metal against him, seeing how their bows and nunchucks would burn instantly. And that was exactly the case. Specifically, sais, arrows and shurikens. All of them cock-shaped. At first setting them ablaze or dodging them by turning into invisible smoke. But then a new idea came to mind. Though controlling metal was not in his Fire roster, he could manipulate the melting point of minerals in general. Which meant they could be liquified and hardened at will. Vic united all the melted minerals to create a giant metal boulder. It was later released upon the Rainbow Ninjas who had no choice but to flee.

STOP

Vic marveled at his ingenious tactic until he was surprised by a Bleach Bomb that was thrown at the boulder to slowly corrode it. And it didn't come from the ninjas. The oxidation also generated a poisonous gas. Moments before fainting, he caught a glimpse of the Yellow City supervillain reflected in the decomposing rock.

PLAY

BREED

The loud punk-driven music from his own tape woke him from his slumber. Vic was tied to a chair in an attic. There was a pretty crystal red woman dressed as a conventional housewife pressing play on his Walkman. She walked away and started setting the table for two. As the alien pondered about using his powers, he saw his flannel shirt hanging in the corner on a coat rack. Vic couldn't help but notice his picture on the television screen in front of him. It was a news broadcast with the headline:

"BOUNTY FOR THE DEVIL JUNKIE ALIEN HOMOPHOBE TERRORIST. FIFTY MILLION BLOOD DOLLAR REWARD OFFERED BY PRESIDENT WOKE!!!!"

Vic shook his head and scoffed in disbelief. Little did he know that, aside from the news, there were Wanted posters with his picture scattered all around the city. Which would bring forth many civilian villains or *Civillains*. While pondering his many calumnious nicknames, the housewife approached him again going for his Walkman.

STOP

— Hi, honey — she said—. Food is ready. You can listen to your music later.

— What the fuck is going on? — Vic asked with misperception—. Who are you?

— You can call me the Housewife from Hell— she said.

— Catchy.

— I made your favorite— she said—. Mac and cheese with roasted potatoes.

— That's not my favorite.

— It will be— she said—. Oh, I assure you... IT WILL BE!

— Before we proceed, are you going to kill me, hand me over for the bounty or rape me... my friend?

— None of the above— she said—. It's complicated.

— Complicated how?

— I want your children— she said—. The alien superpowered lineage.

— I don't have any... oh... I see. And if I say no? I thought raping was out of the question.

— It is— she said—. If you say no, I can make your life a living hell. We clear?

— Crystal clear. Always wanted to say that to you guys.

— That's not all— she said—. I want you to raise them with me. Live in the suburbs. Buy a nice home. White picket fence. You could read the paper in the morning. We could have a dog and a cat. Maybe a hamster. Not sure. Depends on what Junior would want. We would have Thanksgiving dinner at my parent's house where you would tell corny dad jokes. I could be a soccer mom and you could go bowling with your friends. But just a few beers, Mister!

— Okay... I'm starting to see a whole "Misery" scenario playing out here. Was this the "happiness" description or the "make your life a living hell" description?

— YOU FORGOT THE CHRISTMAS PRESENTS FOR THE KIDS! — she said—. I'M GOING TO MURDER YOU! HOW CAN YOU BE SO INSENSITIVE AND SELFISH! ARE YOU INCAPABLE OF SHARING? DO I NEED TO SET A BILLION RULES SO YOU ACKNOWLEDGE WHAT A WORTHLESS PIECE OF SHIT YOU ARE???

— WE HAVE NO CHILDREN! WE DON'T NEED TO BREED EITHER! I DON'T CARE ABOUT THIS WHOLE SYSTEM ORIENTED BULLSHIT!

— Stop yelling, sweetie — she said—. We can work it out. I only need to know where you are at all times, check your phone every hour, destroy your dreams and aspirations, blame you for my failures and, after our children are born, we will stop having sex to honor Jesus. No porn either, darling. Well... maybe just Sex and the City. We can watch all the seasons over and over again. LET'S START NOW! I'LL GO GET THEM!

— NO, PLEASE! STOP!

— What? — she said—. You want your cologne? Of course, dear. BUT EAT YOUR FUCKING DINNER FIRST!

The Housewife from Hell force fed him the Mac and Cheese with roasted potatoes in liquid form. She then took a tank of gas from under the table and covered the alien with it. She left the room and Vic started to squirm in all directions. His chest was bubbling hot and he knew the very idea of being in that relationship would make him explode. Aside from the fact he was about to get burned and would literally blow up. It was time to think fast. Act fast.

Then it came to him. The gasoline. While having the flannel shirt on, he was able to control anything flammable. Maybe even draw the shirt to the combustible agent itself like he linked to the airstream with the purple flannel. Vic closed his eyes and concentrated on the flannel shirt. No other thought. Only the shirt. Bit by bit, the coat rack started moving. Rocking back and forth with telekinetic energy. The Housewife from Hell came in with the first season of Sex and the City in one hand and a blowtorch in the other. Just when she was about to burn him to a crisp, Vic summoned the flannel shirt. It entered his arms quickly; making him glow, burn the chair and ropes while at the same time levitating him with fluorescent scarlet eyes.

PLAY

The Housewife from Hell paused with fear. And out of that fear, she dropped the DVDs and torched the alien. This generated a Fire overdose that, even though it didn't harm him at all, spread the flames to the entire room. Vic could extinguish the flames with his powers, but the attic was humid and poorly ventilated. Which led to a lot of smoke. Though Vic could control this as well, the woman was already suffering from asphyxiation. And despite all the madness she inspired, he wouldn't leave her there to die.

Looking around, two things caught his eye. A video camera that apparently was recording the whole incident and a set of drums against the wall with a Smokey Stover strip sticker saying, "Where there's foo, there's fire." Vic smiled, took the woman in his arms and jumped towards the drum set and the adjacent wall.

— GROHL SMASH! — the alien cried out bursting in flames.

The fire was generated like an atmosphere surrounding him so no harm came to the Civillain when they landed below. Vic extinguished the flames and smoke once he saw she was safe.

STOP

— Are you okay? — Vic asked genuinely concerned.
— Yes— she said—. I'm sorry. I needed the money... the bounty.
— But why torture me? Why not turn me in?

The woman fainted before she could answer. Vic noticed he was in a suburban-like neighborhood that even had a church beside it. But it wouldn't take long for this seemingly ordinary church to become something else entirely.

PLAY

LITHIUM

The Cathedral's foundation started to shift like a Transformer until it turned into a spaceship. Vic couldn't believe his eyes. Especially when said spaceship started to chase him. The alien started running in the opposite direction. His legs were covered in flames and he jumped to continue fleeing through the air. However, the Church Ship was faster and soon caught up to beam him up into the cockpit. Inside there was a preacher with a locomotive hat piloting the religious rocket. Before he could even say anything, Vic was struck with a giant ray gun behind him. It screwed up his Bipolar euthymia in an instant.

STOP

— GOD DAMN IT! — Vic cried out in psychological pain —. WHAT THE FUCK DID YOU JUST DO TO ME?

— QUIET, DEMON! — the preacher screamed—. YOU'RE ONLY GETTING WHAT YOU DESERVE!

— I'M NOT A DEMON!

— Then explain the blasphemy and being covered in Fire.

— Good point... but still. Who are you?

— I am the Holy Engineer. I created this Purity Ray myself to thwart any ill-conceived feelings that stray away from our Maker. Now it has shown me your true colors. And I will rid this world of your satanic influence!

— You don't understand — Vic said starting to weep oceans of tears while his chest blazed with radioactivity—. YOU'RE GOING TO DESTROY US ALL!

— Don't trick me, demon! I know what you are. They say you came from above but I know you came from below!

— I WANT TO KILL MYSELF! YOU GOT TO STOP!

— Far beat it for me to stop you. GO BACK TO HELL!

PLAY

Vic fell to his knees and tried to center himself with Grunge music. There was a similar camera like the one he saw in the Housewife's attic. In his gut he knew it had something to do with President Woke and the bounty on his head. It still made no sense why they wouldn't just turn him in. But then, while listening to the lyrics, it came to him. Religion was going to save him. Not God himself. But the belief. Faith. Opposite to the nihilism and the hopelessness brewed by depression. The need for meaning. A prayer for something that was divine to him. Like the Alternative Valkyrie. And it really worked. But not in the way he had hoped.

STOP

— It's no use resisting — the Holy Engineer boasted—. Not even the Lord himself can save you! This bounty is as good as mine!

— BULLSHIT! — Vic said getting up very euphoric and speaking very fast with an occasional roar—. It's not about God and your salvation, or maybe something even more profound like resonating chambers of the NETHERWORLD, where I cry, I weep, I laugh, I fuck everything, ANYTHING, to breathe, something, CHARCOAL, bloodred smoke rings from HELL. Yes, YES!!! That's how I save myself. Not with the Christian God, Muslim prophets we cannot represent, nothing Krisna, maybe Buddhist, through meditation, reaching my Nirvana, my Bodhisattva, the greatest of Grunge Legends, KURT-FUCKING-COBAIN!!!

— Now I know you've been possessed Demon! I speak your name and cast thee out to fry in the Lake of Fire!

— THEN I'LL COME BACK WITH THE MEAT PUPPETS, MOTHERFUCKER!!!!

PLAY

Vic started to laugh in the peak of his Hessian evil joy. Nevertheless, faith only made him manic and, therefore, his chest was still a bio-hazard waiting to unleash its radioactive turmoil. Focus had to come from his music. And the song name gave him another idea. Since it was possible to control any metal's melting point and state, the alien could separate certain minerals and reconfigure them at will. And this was tested on the Church ship itself. Feeling it out. All the molten metal. Separating itself. And discovering his salvation. The song name.

Lithium. Every Bipolar's dream. Vic chemically engineered the element into an edible morsel and coursed it fast through his burning veins until his chest was at safe levels again. But by doing so, he also crippled the ship itself which went crashing to the ground. Vic managed to stay afloat with his fire thrusters. At the same time, saving the other Civillain bounty hunter from his demise. It was the first time in his superhero career he felt stupid. Why save the assholes? This one fainted as well. But not far from his landing site, a new dilemma presented itself with no chance for a breather.

POLLY

It was a pretty 14-year-old girl being held captive by none other than the Redneck Crystal Posse. She was tied up and carried into a dark warehouse. Vic left the Holy Engineer and ran fast towards the Posse leaving a streak of fire in his tracks. However, his actions were impulsive and he underestimated them by going into the warehouse without warning. As the alien went in, all this became obvious. Having the whole Posse of Civillains surrounding him with the poor girl tied to a chair in the middle.

STOP

— Let her go — Vic said in a serious voice —. It's me you want.

— Told ya, boy — Brody said with a vindictive smirk—. You wasn't gonna be so lucky if I had my druthers.

— I get it. But you don't need the girl. If it's about getting me back for before or the bounty on my head, I'll gladly turn myself in if you release her.

— Relax, alien. I'm just a Friend. Ain't that right, sugar?

— My name is Pauline! — the girl cried out bravely.

— Polly? — the Redneck leader replied comically —. Polly wanna cracker? Reckon you need to be housebroken and yer wings need to be cut off, bitch. You're in my cage now. And we gonna gang-bang you like mashing them taters.

— Over my dead body — Vic intervened.

— Oh, but that's the whole idea, alien— Brody continued—. I can even narrate for ya. How we gonna be riding the slut. And not the trolley kind. We be burning her meat and slicing her pretty little skin off.

— Sounds boring — Pauline remarked.

— SHUT YOUR YAPPER, WHORE!

— You call her a whore again and I will turn you into a flaming eunuch — the superhero assured him.

— But ain't you the fudgepacker type? Y'all gay folk should be exterminated like Jews in them camps. There be songs written bout' it.

— Strike three, motherfucker. Now you're gonna get it. Do yourself a favor, you waste of sperm and eggs wannabe plankton Klu Klux Hick. Don't go to any rock shows and don't buy any more records.

— Well then, poop or get off the pot, fag. I may could be darn happy like a puppy with two peckers to see you become a real man.

— GLADLY! — Vic responded setting ablaze.

PLAY

Moments before the superhero could unleash any attack, Brody drew a freeze gun and covered him in a block of ice up to his neck. Vic immediately started to radiate heat but the temperature that covered him was near Absolute Zero. Which meant it was advanced Black Silence Tech. Though his fire powers kept him alive, the lack of kinetic energy of such stillness prevented him from melting the ice with a chemical reaction. And though both his powers and the room temperature surrounding him would swap heat signatures to liberate him in due course, it wouldn't be enough time to save Pauline from getting raped. A dark experience he had to stomach from the very first moment one of the Rednecks ripped off a piece of her clothing.

It was making him sick. Extremely sick. And not in the sensitivity sense. But in the nuclear sense. His chest was turning all colors. He just could not bear witness to such an atrocity. Vic apologized in his thoughts to all the women of the universe for the crimes perpetrated by his own gender. But the answer was in front of him the whole time. Radioactivity was still possible at those temperatures. All he needed was enough thermal radiation to create the necessary fusion meltdown of the core. Aside from his own powers, he took the fire of the flame throwers intended to torch Pauline to a crisp. And that gave him enough time to melt the ice, take Pauline and run out of there.

END SIDE 1. TAPE SWITCH. SIDE 2.

PLAY

TERRITORIAL PISSINGS

Vic needed Grunge to center his emotions. After having switched the tape, he propelled himself to the skies with Pauline in his arms. The alien was very careful, as with the Civillain Housewife, not to burn her while streaking through the air in the enclosed red-tinted dome. Oddly, the dome walls were filled with many non-artsy graffities. They were all signed by the Redneck Crystal Posse and glorified all types of hate crimes against minorities, Jewish and LGBTIQA+ people. As Vic reflected on how the Posse could ever reach such heights, the explanation came to him by turning his head and seeing it with his own eyes. All of them had jetpacks armed with heat-seeking missiles. Which was unfortunate for his current powers.

Though the impact of said missiles might be endured by him, they would definitely kill Pauline. At least it's what the alien thought at first. But trying to control the Fire in the missiles and the jetpacks, Vic realized they were all powered by the same Absolute Zero technology. Which meant that, not only could he not control or melt their gear, but he could also be petrified by Ice upon impact and would die just the same.

By gazing into Pauline's scared eyes, Vic perceived something else. Wisdom perhaps. Maybe all societies problems had to do with copying everybody else. Trying to fit in. Be cool. Be somebody. Even if that somebody is evil. Full-on Identity Crisis. That's all it took. There were surely good individuals amongst the extremists. But the lack of an ideology makes one susceptible to belong. To form groups. Then comes territory. Turf wars. And those left out in resentment, destroy everything and everybody out of rage. Which was the major issue with the clones. Fortunately, Vic didn't care about belonging, vendettas or public opinion. He would always be an alien to them. So, why worry? There was a job to be done. A purpose. Nothing more.

As for his current predicament, Vic started to zig-zag through the air trying to lose the several Ice missiles on his tail but realized it wouldn't be enough to escape from them all. However, the superhero discovered he could multiply himself in flame form. So, he resourcefully created many Fire Avatars of himself flying in different directions. This was a neat trick to draw their heat-seeking missiles away while at the same time exhausting the Redneck jetpack ammo. The plan was to fight back once Pauline was safe. Something that could be done by floating her momentarily in a hot air current while unleashing his ultimate attack. And it couldn't have come at a better time. Brody was closing in with a jetpack of his own and two huge Ice missiles pointed at them.

— NOVOSELIC, GET TOGETHER! — Vic screamed launching Pauline in the hot air current while harnessing a humongous fireball— KAME ...HAME ...DOOOOKEN!

Brody and the remaining rednecks were all scorched in one blast. Vic caught Pauline in his arms shortly after. The evaporated deaths of his foes even erased all the graffities in the red crystal. Leaving the dome spotless. Made whole. As it should be. The superhero left Pauline by the side of the road and returned to the skies shortly after. He looked back for a moment and saw her mouth the words, "THANKS!"

The alien was pleased he was able to prevent the raping from ever taking place... to know she could be saved. In some way wanting to go back in time and averting the initial kidnapping so she had no memory of it all. But Pauline was safe now. That's all that mattered.

DRAIN YOU

Vic couldn't find a moment's peace. Since seconds later, he was sucked into a giant vacuum cleaner atop a skyscraper. Before going in, he could see a live Crystal Red Chim-Chim Monkey with electrodes connected to his brain and a Walkman much like his own on his back. The destination was a room with crystal glass surrounded by absolute darkness.

STOP

— What the fuck is this? — Vic asked to the nothingness around him—. Where am I? Who stopped my tape?

— I did — a deep voice answered through his own headphones.

— Are you the weird monkey from before?

— I am. And I assure you, there's nothing weird about me.

— A telepathic Crystal Monkey sucking me into a giant vacuum cleaner? It's pretty weird, dude.

— I mean, it won't sound so weird once I explain my origins as a mere lab animal being experimented on. These experiments had to do with music. After a while, I managed to understand radio waves in a way nobody could. Tuning into a person's mind... their very soul. This "vacuum cleaner" as you call it is really a virtual reality containment unit where I can tap in to your mind. Bending it at my will.

— Yeah, still seems weird.

— Well, it is what it is.

— Let me skip ahead here. You're going to torture me, right?

— Yes.

— This bounty makes no sense.

— You really think the bounty has to do with turning you in? No, no, no. We are meant to drive you insane. And with the blood money I'll get with my results, I will be able to control all of you.

— You do realize that if I go insane, I'll explode, we all die and you won't get shit?

— As much as I would like to believe that, you'll say just about anything to save your neck. Now you will know what it's like to be experimented on. And everybody will remember the name DEVOLUTIONIZER!!!

— Oh, that's not weird. Kind of like the bunny with the batteries but you're a toy ape with evolution. Makes sense.

— NO! THERE'S NO BUNNY! MY NAME IS ORIGINAL!

— Sure, it is. Are you going and going and going anywhere with this?

— Enough talk. I'll be draining your emotions now. Soon you'll be nothing but a fucked up lobotomized husk!

— NO, WAIT!!!

A high pitch frequency attacked Vic's hearing as if a hornet nest was pumped into his ear canal. The noise took him down to his knees in pain and his first impulse was to take his headphones off.

PLAY

But it stopped unexpectedly before he could do it. Even hearing his music again, the alien was suddenly in a different scenario. High school. A physics class with many human kids his age. Something was off. Specifically, a blonde Davanita sitting three rows across from him wearing just a bikini. Her mere existence could kill him. As if he knew exactly what was coming. The strange part was the series of flashforwards experienced from then on.

Vic in Grunge clothing talking to an alternative-rock Davanita in the hall. She appeared to show little interest. Or none whatsoever. Laughing at him with her friends.

Vic comes home to find his father beating his mother. He locks himself in his room hearing her screams. Vic cries.

Davanita at a party surrounded by many macho-guys hitting on her. Vic in the corner watching this happen, alone and sad.

Valentine's day. Vic giving Davanita roses and chocolates. She receives them with a weird look then throws them in the trash once he leaves. Vic notices and picks them up.

Vic coming home to find her mother with many bruises and bleeding from her nose. Vic gives her the roses and chocolates. She smiles with tears in her eyes.

Vic asks Davanita out on a date. She agrees but only wants him for the ride. She ditches him once they reach her desired destination.

Davanita and her friends check out a muscular jock bench-pressing. Vic covets from behind.

Vic working out at the gym. He takes a handful of vitamins. Pees extremely yellow moments later.

Vic comes home to find his father beating his mother again. Psyched up because of his exercises, he decides to fight him. His father beats him as well.

Davanita agrees to go out on another date. She talks all the time. He focuses on her lips that mouth the words "YOU'RE A GOOD FRIEND."

Davanita making out with a buff tattoo-covered hair band musician. Vic crying in a dark alley outside.

Vic expressing his love to Davanita in the park. She shakes her head. Her lips read, "MAYBE IN THE FUTURE... BUT NOT NOW."

In a tree, a mother bird is regurgitating food for her infant chick. Vic is crying with his back to the tree trunk below.

LOUNGE ACT

*V*ic *down on one knee in front of a redheaded Davanita. Both of them are in their forties. He proposes and she accepts crying. They hug and they kiss.*

Spring. Vic and Davanita are getting married in a simple ceremony by the ocean shore. A fat bald priest dressed in white with glasses stands between them. Vic kisses Davanita once the priest stops talking.

Summer. Vic and Davanita eating breakfast and talking with joy.

Fall. Vic and Davanita eating breakfast. Only Vic is talking with joy. Davanita seems bored.

Winter. Vic and Davanita eating breakfast. Both are serious and silent. Concentrated on their own food without even looking at each other.

Vic having dinner with Davanita and her male friend, John. He's wearing a leather jacket and looks exactly like Black Silence without the mohawk. John appears to be telling a joke and she can't stop laughing. Vic just sits there serious and consumed with jealousy. His hands are wrapped around a knife on the table. He's shivering. As if trying to contain himself.

Vic checking his watch. It's 2:15am. He's pacing nervously and takes out his cell phone. There's an unanswered message of "WHERE ARE YOU???" from 6pm. Davanita walks in drunk and disheveled. Vic yells at her and she just walks by with indifference.

Vic smelling Davanita's bottled perfume. Davanita and John speaking in the kitchen. Vic smells John's leather jacket. Closes his eyes in pain. Cries covering his face.

Vic yelling at Davanita while throwing plates against the wall. Davanita leaves without so much as a tear. Vic leans against the closed door and cries again.

Vic buys drugs from a Dealer that looks exactly like Mister H.

Vic starts shooting heroin for the first time and falls back unconscious.

Vic walking in the street with a deranged and intoxicated look on his face. He enters an apartment building, takes out a knife and knocks on one of the doors. John answers. Vic thrusts the knife at his head. John intercepts the attack grabbing his wrist. He smiles. John turns into Black Silence. Vic realizes the knife has also turned into a syringe.

Vic wakes up in his apartment after being stoned a long time. He opens the door. Mister H grabs his head with his glowing palm.

Vic wakes up in his apartment after being stoned a long time. He opens the door. Mister H grabs his head with his glowing palm.

Vic wakes up in his apartment after being stoned a long time. He opens the door. Mister H grabs his head with his glowing palm.

Vic wakes up in his apartment after being stoned a long time. He takes a gun out of a drawer and puts it in his mouth. He shoots himself.

Vic wakes up in his apartment after being stoned a long time. He's surrounded by four cassette tapes and a Walkman. Just moments after getting up, Feminazi starts to strangle him in his bed. Black Silence and Mister H are in the background laughing.

STOP

— NOOOOOOO! — Vic screamed after appearing alone again with withdrawal symptoms in his apartment.

— Vic? — a kid said in voice over mode.

— Danny? Is that you?

— And me — a girl spoke.

— Pauline?

— Yes. We're both here. Devolutionizer won't be bothering you anymore. We tied him up and took off his mind control tech. That's how we're speaking to you now.

— Is this real or am I in a different circle of the Underworld?

— We're totally real. Whatever goes on inside isn't. So don't believe anything you see in there.

— It's not that easy. Everything seems so lifelike. As if I actually had the experiences I'm remembering.

— Danny explained it to me before. They're not memories. Devolutionizer used your real memories to recreate an alternate reality.

— Just please get me the fuck out of here.

— I'm afraid that part is a bit more complex.

— Complex?

— It's as if you're trapped in a nightmare you need to wake up from.

— Okay... and how exactly do I do that?

— It may sound corny, but think "happy thoughts."

— How can I wake up from a fucked-up nightmare to a happy-wet dream? That doesn't make any sense.

— It makes perfect sense— Danny intervened with an intellectual tone—. The standing waves opposite of the zinc spheres inside the vacuum and the monkey's pack create the frequency adjusted to your mental state, meaning getting sucked in and out would be as an electromagnetic wave passing through copper wire among a dipole resonator. Of course, this mechanism has the additional factor of virtual reality linked to emotional states. Translated into physics as ordinary positive and negative charges.

— So... happy thoughts?

— Yeah, happy thoughts.

— Got it. Now I know you're real. There's no chance in Hell that I could have that information lodged in my subconscious.

Vic started to concentrate but it was harder that it appeared to be. Being Bipolar made him question what happiness even looked like. There was no way to imagine anything good with Davanita after what had happened. Nor could he envision himself being liked and honored by all. The alien only wanted to be left alone.

Maybe that was what happiness was all about. Being in his own planet. Eighteen again. Without humans. Only nature and small magical creatures called Melvins. A children's story his mother used to read to him. Spawning and maintaining all the ecosystem around him in pure perfection. He would live in a cabin. Alone. With just books, videogames and movies for company. Grunge music playing all day long and a Seven Eleven run by a robot.

After daydreaming about his hermit paradise, Vic suddenly felt a gush of wind. Escalating until becoming a full-on hurricane. The virtual reality faded to black and the alien found himself flying through a tube and spit out into the Seattle rain where his flight powers were immediately activated. Over the vacuum were Danny and Pauline stood patiently. They had the monkey's gizmos on their heads while the Civillain himself was tied up at their feet.

— Thanks a lot, you two — Vic said flattered—. Really appreciate you helping me out. It's very rare for me.

— You saved us —Danny said bashfully —. It's the least we could do. I checked the virtual reality archives. It's impressive that you could still manage to be this sane after everything he put you through.

— Well, everybody has made the dumbass mistake of allowing me to listen to Grunge while they torture me. Almost lost it at the end, though. I really owe my sanity to you guys. Thanks for the telepathic pep talk.

— No problem — Pauline said smiling —. You're our hero. And we will be on your side always. Unfortunately, I can't say the same for the rest of the Red City...

— I'm starting to sense something's afoot — Vic said with suspicion.

— Go to the Hill. You can see for yourself.

— Which hill?

— Capitol Hill.

— What is it this time? Orcs and leprechauns?

— Yeah no, it's a Gay Pride Parade.

— So? I have no beef with that.

— But they do have a beef with you — Danny added.

— Oh right— Vic said scoffing—. Forgot about my bad rep as a devil junkie alien homophobe terrorist.

— Don't forget pederast?

— WHAT?!

— It's new.

— That's so stupid. I'm basically a kid myself! Aside from the fact I would never do such a thing. Don't tell me. You're the ones I supposedly abused?

— Yep — Pauline answered—. Ironic, isn't it?

— Extremely— Vic agreed.

— We can go with you and disprove all this.

— No need. I know exactly what to do. Get to safety. If I need you, I'll holler.

— You got it! — both of them responded joyfully.

PLAY

STAY AWAY

Vic flew to Capitol Hill and landed a mile away from the Gay Pride Parade mentioned by his friends. It was even worse than expected. Aside from the sheer volume of people waving pride flags and their lynch-oriented expressions, the superhero was meant to fight the very people he swore to defend. To that adding the army of Rainbow Ninjas in the back. But the strangest part was a Tyrannosaurus-like quake and a chant he could barely make out over his music.

STOP

The quake and chants grew louder with a chorus going "WOKE! WOKE! WOKE!" The rumble on the ground was now accompanied by a thunder-driven sound. Something big was coming. And this time there was no Golem to fight back. Awaiting anxiously with suspense in his heart, the source finally revealed itself turning from a perpendicular stand point. It was a giant lizard android mimicked to look like Godzilla. But it was also shining in all the colors of the rainbow, had an afro, a Mexican sombrero, a Muslim burka, Jewish muttonchops, a rosary necklace, a mace shaped like a mop, thick-wool baby booties and both male and female reproductive organs.

— Grandma take me home — Vic said to himself in astonishment.

— Howdy — said an amplified voice coming from the beast in a more refined redneck southern accent—. Reckon you're going' to Hell in a handbasket, varmint.

— I believe you.

— WE CAN'T HEAR YOU! — a gay man shouted throwing him a megaphone.

Vic picked it up and spoke through the bullhorn:

— I imagine it's President Woke speaking from inside that PC abomination.

— Indeed — President Woke answered —. And this here reptile whatchamacallit is called a Progressaurus. My fortress, my weapon and the means to yer end.

— Speaking of end, does that thing take a shit? Is that where zoomers come from?

— Wise cracks ain't gonna save your skin.

— Let's get serious then. I have a message for the Red People.

— Go right ahead. Won't help them minds, though.

— You think? Do they know what you're really trying to do?

— Lord willin' and the Creek won't rise, you'll lose your marbles before they ever find out.

— Well, I'll spell it out for them: People of Red City! Your president has been lying to you! Not only am I not all the things he claims I am, but the bounty on my head for me to lose my head has a hidden purpose behind it. The radioactive device you see glowing on my chest will go off if I go mad. So, there is no reward or future for the winner. Only a nuclear holocaust. He plans to kill you all as all the life in Window World! OH AND GOD IS GAY!

— So, why ain't you gay yourself? Why create y'all heterosexuals?

— To reproduce. You're not very bright, are you?

— HE INSULTED PRESIDENT WOKE! — a lesbian shouted.

— AND HE'S A LIAR! — a bisexual man added.

— HUMMINA, HUMMINA! — screeched a transnational non-binary man that identified as a female Cicada from the Blue Zone.

— He ain't lying — President Woke answered with indifference —. I'm blowing up a storm in his pretty peach of a chest.

The crowd grew silent following the President's words. Moments after, a panic started and they all fled scattered through the adjacent streets. In the end, it was only him against the Progressaurus and the Rainbow Ninja army.

— I'm surprised you told them the truth — Vic said through his megaphone —. You really don't give a shit about them, do you?

— No siree bob — President Woke answered through his voice enhanced mechanical beast—. But that ain't the reason I told them. Fact is, you're gonna blow yer top one way or the other. It's just a matter of time, boy. Didn't really need a bounty.

— Your overconfidence and underestimating me is your weakness.

— Heavens to Betsy, varmint— Woke said while displaying a red sphere in the android's chest—. It appears the porch light's on but nobody's home. Cain't never beat you machine to flannel shirt. That's why, contrary to my fellow clone brothers, I ain't taking no chances from the git-go. DOOM ORB... PLAY K-POP!

— AH, SHOOT THE SHIT.

Without hesitation, the Progressaurus jumped over the Rainbow Ninjas and landed in front of the alien. The beast kicked the weak and powerless Vic Grunge before he could even realize what was happening.

— KICK IS GOOD! — President Woke yelled followed by an evil laugh.

The force was so strong, Vic ended up crashing all the way up in Renton. Specifically, in Greenwood Cemetery. As luck would have it, the distance gave him a few seconds to mildly heal warming his body tissue and turn on his flying powers to break his fall. The horrible K-Pop music could still be heard, therefore, weakening him and turning off his flannel shortly after. Which could only mean the Progressaurus was closing in. Something that wasn't surprising seeing how quickly it moved before. Vic had to find some place to lay low while coming up with a new offensive tactic.

The solution presented itself in a strange manner. The Jimi Hendrix memorial that everybody knew as a tomb of the GOAT guitarist, was an open night club to the alien's eyes. The name "27 CLUB" was glowing on top in pink neon and the bouncer was none other than Jim Morrison dressed in black with aviator shades reading Aldus Huxley. Vic approached the esteemed rock singer as he stood by the Doors.

— Are you who I think you are? — Vic said enthusiastically —. You're a Rock God!

— No— Jim Morrison said in a poetic trippy vibe—. Being a god would imply I'm eternal. And I am the End.

— As well as the beginning.

— What?

— You're the doorman. And doors are always the beginning of something.

— I think you mean there are things known and things unknown and in between are the doors. Just as the highest and lowest points are the important ones. Anything else is just... in between.

— Yeah, that sounds better.

— Of course it does.

— May I go in through the known and unknown to the highest and lowest points of the universe, Mister Morrison?

— I have to see some ID.

— Ah, c'mon!

— Sorry, club rules.

— I don't have an ID. I'm an illegal alien. Literally. Besides... I'm 18.

— I can't let you in then. Your death certificate must state you're 27. No more, no less.

— Death certificate?

— You are dead, aren't you?

— I don't think so. I know because I can still hear the K-Pop. Something I'm pretty sure can't materialize in the afterlife.

— Sadly, I can hear it too.

— Well, I do feel extremely weak. Is that a death thing?

— Can't really say. I really think death made me stronger.

— So, what now?

— Go back and face what you're running from. Expose yourself to your deepest fear; after that, fear has no power, and the fear of freedom shrinks and vanishes. You are free.

— Bitch, please. We're talking about K-Pop here.

— Right... why would anybody play this crap to begin with?

— Let's just say shitty music takes away my flaming superpowers. Maybe you can help me.

— Help you how?

— Light my fire?

— Seriously? It's not even one of mine!

— All apologies. What will it take then?

— Get me some bourbon. It won't get me drunk now that I'm dead but it will piss the shit out of Jimi and Janice.

— You don't get along?

— Nope. A lot of bad history. Hence me being out here.

— Why not leave then?

— Where's the fun in that? I have the soul of a clown. I need to make people question their reality. Like you, for instance. You actually believed I was the bouncer.

— Well smack me hard and call me a bitch. I bought your whole act!

— I know. You may go in, by the way. It's an elevator.

— You mean I don't have to break on through?

— What?

— People are strange down there, aren't day?

— Stop it.

— Sorry. Can't help myself.

— It's okay. At least the songs are mine this time. But I must warn you... with nothing more than an American Prayer, only a Ghost Song remains.

— Are you being serious or is it a pun against my previous puns?

Jim Morrison smiled in silence and continued to read his book. Vic hesitated for a moment then entered the center of the memorial. The stone guitar had an elevator button to go down. He pressed it and descended into the ground floor which opened its doors to a 60's nostalgia bar. There the alien saw Brian Jones playing darts, Janice Joplin and Amy Winehouse singing karaoke duets with perfect harmonics while Jimi Hendrix himself was all the way in the back. For a moment it made him question having survived the reptile kick. Jimi was on the floor with his back against the wall while improvising solos on his guitar. To a point of actually improving the karaoke music and somehow fusing it with the K-Pop. Vic walked directly to him in his weakened state, unseen by all the other 27 Club members. The Grunge enthusiast couldn't help but look in all directions. As if he was searching for someone who wasn't there.

— Excuse me— Vic apologized bumping into Robert Johnson who appeared out of nowhere.

— Think nothing of it— Robert Johnson responded—. He's waiting for you, you know?

— He is?

— Clock is ticking. It's almost over.

— What's almost over?

Robert Johnson smiled and kept on walking. Vic pretended the conversation never took place and approached Hendrix.

— Hey Jimi — Vic said as if he belonged—. Nice place you got here.

— Do I know you, man? — Jimi said with indifference while he continued playing.

— Well... no. Jim let me in. I confess I'm 18. And I'm alive. At least I think I am... my radioactive chest being my only proof.

— Don't worry. You're alive. If you were dead and 27, Jim wouldn't have let you in. He's like that. I knew he wouldn't make a good bouncer.

— Goddamn you, Morrison.

— What?

— Nothing... fact is, I really need your help, Mister Hendrix.

— In what way?

— I'm the Grunge Rock Alien. Or so I am called around these parts. I come from a different time period. I'm also a rocker but somewhat different from what you are accustomed to.

— Oh yeah. Kurt's music. I'm familiar.

— Yes, Kurt... Cobain... is he here? IS HE HERE????!!!!

— Relax, Grunge Rock Groupie. He ain't here. Every 27 Club tomb is a bar on its own. Except for Kurt's. Since he was cremated, there's no physical Club under his tutelage. Drawn to this astral plane thanks to a small recreation of his Memorial Park in the Red City He keeps to himself mostly. Never showing up to the rest of the clubs and not letting anybody know his whereabouts. Such a shame. I really like him.

— What does he do?

— Nobody knows. Pretty much Stays Away.

— What about Jim?

— We have a love-hate relationship. I never ban him from the clubs because he would only show up out of spite. I do respect him though. We're just very different people. He loves teasing us and I'm sick of being used as a prop. Especially his obsession with sucking my dick.

— Excuse me?

— Not literally, of course. He only pretends to do it to piss me off.

— But... why?

— Don't ask.

— Makes me think Jim's 27 Club is deserted all the time.

— Are you kidding? It's in Paris! I can stomach Jim's fake blow jobs to be jamming in the Pere Lachaise.

— Okay, I have to ask now because it's driving me crazy. Where the fuck is Window World France, Mexico, Southern USA and so on? I imagine there's a Window World UK for the graves of Amy and Brian.

— You do realize Window World is a planet and has another side?

— Oh! Another side... of course! I knew I felt some different vibes when digging in the Yellow City. So, it's kind of like China to the States.

— Precisely. Except here the Seattle version is the side you already know and the other side is composed by many countries of Earth admired by the Crystal People assorted in one very large city. Colors are mixed as well.

— Are they assholes on the other side too?

— Yeah, man. Either they think they're better than everyone in the Seattle zone or they humbly want to cross to this side and become assholes when they do.

— That's a damn shame.

— They also celebrate weird rituals with giant eggs. Have them in their homes and worship them like gods. Never hung around long enough to see what came out.

— Exactly what this story was missing. Xenomorphs. That's fucking great.

— Don't follow.

— Aliens.

— Like you?

— Never mind.

— So, what can I do you for?

— You're gonna help me?

— I assume that terrible music from outside has something to do with you. And I'll help in any way that I can if it stops entirely.

— Fortunately, that's exactly what needs to happen. That music takes away my Fire powers. It comes from a Doom Orb in the heart of an intersexual dinosaur robot who's guarded by an army of Rainbow Ninjas.

— Did you really just say that or did I drop some acid without knowing?

— I shit you not, man. Not even LSD can whip up something so fucked up. It's my everyday reality.

— Well, you sold me. And I know exactly how to help.

— I'm listening...

— I have Fire powers of my own. Napalm. Bound to the Viet Nam War of my time. I'll burn my guitar and it will inherit said powers for you to fight all that crap you just mentioned.

— I can't let you burn your guitar. I mean... it's Jimi Hendrix's guitar! A legendary Rock God instrument! No fucking way!!!

— It's okay. I love my guitar. And you sacrifice the things you love. Once you inherit my Napalm Strat, you must simply play any chord and point it at his heart... her heart... what is the correct way here?

— Don't bother. I got it. Do you think it will work?

— As sure as mud in Woodstock, kid.

— Awesome.

— Any message for Kurt?

— Yeah... please tell him... thanks.

— You got it. Now, let's get this groove started.

Jimi got up and played a quick rendition of the Star-Spangled Banner. Moments after, he took off his guitar and lit it on fire. The GOAT kneeled and started to make strange Chaman-like movements until the flames covered the entire instrument. He then got sucked into the guitar itself. Vic was speechless throughout the whole ritual. As the flaming Napalm Strat lay on the ground, the superhero picked it up and raised it into the air like a videogame sword. Robert Johnson was gone. And none of the other 27 Club members ever looked at him. The alien proceeded to exit the tomb through the elevator. Jim was no longer outside. The Progressaurus and the Rainbow Ninjas were waiting for him in the cemetery.

Without a moment's hesitation, Vic slammed the guitar into the ground twice. It wasn't a random attack. It was calculated from the start. The napalm created a fire trail on opposite sides leaving a straight line in the middle where he could reach President Woke's moving beast fortress without so much interference from the ninjas. Even affected physically, the alien ran as fast as he could. Protected from their long-range attacks except for those in the central section who were eliminated with a Napalm Strat thrust. Strangely, all the ninjas would evaporate upon contact as if they were not made of Crystal at all. The Progressaurus then spit out a ball of water. Vic dodged it and struck the guitar aiming at the beast's heart. Jimi Hendrix came out in his ghostly aura taking the red Doom Orb with him to the zenith.

— EXCUSE ME — Jimi called out as he disappeared in the ozone—, WHILE I KISS THE SKY!

PLAY

Vic strapped the Napalm Strat to his back, smiled at the Rainbow Ninjas and started unleashing his Fire powers once again. The Progressaurus was not responding after the Hendrix attack and was temporarily out of commission. Which gave the alien a great advantage to wipe them all out. Fireballs, dragon breath, flame punches, explosions and heat attacks of all sorts ended the fight in a few minutes. But still... no bodies. All of them just evaporated without a trace.

ON A PLAIN

As the alien continued to theorize about their disappearance, some droplets stood still in the air as if paused by a higher power. The Seattle rain and the water inside the Progressaurus slowly started to merge. They appeared to be coming together in one figure. A man. A fat bald man. Dressed in a white suit. He wore Coke bottle glasses that magnified his deep-blue-sea-colored eyes. However, Vic fixated on the fact the supervillain showed up out of nowhere. It didn't take him long to boast about his own superpowers.

STOP

— I love the smell of Fender in the morning — Vic said spiritedly while drawing his Rock N' Roll sword —. Smells like... a jaguar pouncing on a mustang.

— Probably feeling madder than a wet hen — President Woke said with an evil smile —. Wondering about them false ninjas and my hydro-powers.

— Actually, it makes perfect sense. A supervillain materializing from Seattle rain? About fucking time!

— You a pussy, boy? Ain't nothing but a few sprinkles. Poor in comparison to my full potential. Reckon yer fire gee-tar won't help once my liquid cuts out the flame.

— I'm telling you this right now, Shamu. I'm not sitting in the Splash Zone.

— Always the kidder. Don't really matter where you sit. You 'bout to get drowned.

— Like your gay minions were supposed to drown me? It's an effective trick. I'll give you that. But I'm not impressed.

— What if I done told you the human body might could reach up to 70% water and yer daddy had more ambitious plans for me? Thinking bout' perfection in liketa the highest concentration. Skin being as a crawfish shell blended in a stew. With osmosis at my fingertips to absorb and create what I dang please as solid mass through light refraction.

— Refraction? Oh, Rainbow Ninjas. Now I get it! I knew that kiss tasted like pure Gay Pride in a wet T-shirt. What I don't get is why you planned to destroy the whole planet.

— Because I don't believe in nothing, varmint. I was elected by them Red folk 'cause of my PC agenda. And was finer than a frog hair split four ways. Street wars with them RCP and my rainbow ninjitsu was all it took to bring them together and rile them up. What do you say to that?

— I say fuck your Woke culture. It's not bringing people together. It's driving them apart. People are not thinking about their rights or being special. They're forming groups of their own to condemn anybody who's not a part of them. That's what's really destroying the world. You don't have to make me explode to see it all go up in flames.

— True... but it's much more fun to kill y'all.

— I knew you weren't impartial in this. Were the Rednecks other water constructs or did you generate them out of your own fermented piss?

— Rednecks had my own water coursing through their crystal bodies. Able to control them thoughts only by drinking my tap water self. Manipulating them Red folk likewise. Too easy, I reckon. Is why I might could got killed with boredom. Eventually, this here life of mine had no meaning. None of y'all have any value. Withering away with all them dreams sunk in a bucket of conformity. Day to day habit without doggone feelings to decorate yer sad little ol' lives. Y'all had to die for all this to make right sense.

— As somebody who comes from musical nihilism, I can tell you everything you're saying is bullshit. Nothingness is the meaning. Because it's not handed to you. You must fight and create it from the pit of doom that you're born into. The meaning of life is to turn that nothing into something. The fact that you don't get that makes you both lazy and stupid.

— Now hold yer horses, son. You been the one being innocent. When worn slap out, that something created over yonder will return with Hell's fury to make you plumb-crazy. Y'all may get gussied up for life, but soon y'all be a rooster one day and a feather duster the next.

— So, you don't believe in anything woke? Do you even have one of the LGBTIQA+ identities?

— Cain't never could no more— the villain said taking out his humongous water cock he later unhinged and started swinging as a whip —. Having myself divided between them macho rednecks while opposite to gay ninjas, added to the many sexual identities drinking my water, done left me lost like last year's Easter Egg. Airing my paunch of emotions and not having no feelings whatsoever. My emptiness aside, I still would reconsider being one of them asexual types. But no identity compares to the fulfilment of whipping yer ass, boy!

— All the pieces are coming together. Projecting your emotions and your personality transformed you into the nihilist prick that you are. You don't believe in nothing nor do you care about anything. That's why you didn't mind when the Red People discovered your plans. You could just brainwash them at any time if everything went south. Nevertheless, asexual means no sex. So bring it on, dickless.

PLAY

Though the Napalm Strat had no longer Jimi's spirit or flames, it was recharged by the alien's own firepower. Vic smashed the unbreakable guitar on the ground unleashing a flaming streak towards his opponent. The nihilist supervillain whipped the Fire into steam. The hero then proceeded to use the guitar as a flamethrower which President Woke blocked by reshaping his whip into a wave-like shield. Woke then created more Rainbow Ninjas to ambush the alien from both flanks. Vic defended himself by generating fire avatars of his own to ward off their attacks. President Woke then gathered the Seattle raindrops to create a solid Water Saber.

The supervillain knew both him and the alien were more vulnerable by cloning themselves. In fact, having himself divided between the Red People, the Rednecks and the Ninjas not only left him emotionless, but also much less powerful. Especially regarding the Rainbow Ninjas since his personality was altered severely in full water constructs; unlike the Rednecks who were Crystal and had the same traits as him. But Woke had bad weather to his advantage. Hence the sword fight that took place. Napalm Strat against Water Saber. Steam coming from the clashing blows. But after a while of dueling, the supervillain decided to take a different approach. The ground began to shake. Which made the alien question his surroundings.

STOP

Discontinuing his music to listen accurately, it was already too late. Geysers started erupting from the ground randomly. The clear superiority of Water over Fire ended with Vic losing to a strong spring that put him out and rendered him unconscious. However, he wouldn't wake up in the battlefield where the fight took place.

As Vic came to, he was underwater in a deep pool of some sort. Fully clothed, no Walkman and many cables connected to his head, mouth, nose and ears. There were also chains bounding him to that very spot. Many babies swam chasing dollar bills around him. Like sharks chasing bloody chum. In front of him stood the anarchic president in the interior of a dry room. What really surprised him was not the fact that he could breathe underwater with the noticeable scuba gear in his nose, but that he could actually speak to his enemy through advanced tech showing up as a transcript in the latter's TV screen.

— What the fuck is going on? — Vic said realizing he could be heard.

— Now, now — President Woke said smiling and hearing the robotic voice transmitting the alien's words out loud—. Seems yer only getting a nudge in the right direction. The nuclear kind.

Electric charges passed through Vic's body bringing him a great deal of pain. Both physically and emotionally.

— YOU MOTHERFUCKING PIECE OF SHIT!!! — Vic yelled through the robot transcription.

— That ain't PC language — Woke said laughing—. Reckon y'all Window World dwellers will suffer in what's left of your H-Bomb ticker. And Grunge music ain't gonna save yer rump this time.

— You know you're gonna kill yourself as well?

— Doubt it, varmint. Ain't nothing that can right destroy water. Changes itself and others just the same. You think yer pain comes from piddling dern cables, right? Well, it really comes from the commode doohickey you sauteed in. Being human, it may could have taken me longer to brainwash and guide yer noggin towards suicide. Oh, and speaking of boiled taters, yer powers ain't gonna work while you're in mine.

— Do I dare ask what's up with the Aquababies?

— Clones for the future... but that there tale is for another day.

— Brainwashing since birth, are we?

— No siree.' But I may could brainwash anybody to feel or think what I darn please by them having a cold sip of my almighty self. Out of all the emotions and capital sins against our Lord, greed is my all-time favorite. Richer'n Croesus. You may could have the strongest creed tied up in dern religion, politics, race and sexual orientation, but stacks and coinage can right control y'all till the cows come home.

— Yeah, and you're so fat, that if a cow sent you an invitation to attend a wedding reception in her home, it would tell you to bring a minus-one.

— Joke if you must, alien. Already won.

— Don't think so. You underestimate the Red People. Free will is the variable that fucks up both heavenly and diabolical plans. It's what makes sentient beings unique to choose their freedom. Just ask Black Silence.

— Yet Silence wanted full control over y'all. Only works if them Red folk believed in the illusion of choice. That's why I cain't control them a hundred percent. Best way to manipulate canaries is to make them think they ain't in a cage. Only needed a PC Agenda to fuel their pride. Why do you think yer bounty was so popular? Many knew they could die or that the fight had to do with liberal propaganda instead of them avaricious tendencies. Any dogma is cattywampus once you drink some greed water, boy. All beliefs in a buggy to be cashed out as NOTHING!

— Sorry to tell you this, but money means shit to me. And pain is my religion. You have no leverage to make me crack, your Wokeness. Go ahead and shock me all you want.

— Perhaps you're right. Maybe pain ain't gonna make you piss your druthers. But perhaps pleasure might could. Liketa as the one given to you by Mister H.

— You wouldn't...

— Oh, but I may could. Let's spike them punch and give you some old fashioned H2O with a kick of prescription granny cough syrup.

— NOOOO!

Shortly after his silent scream, President Woke injected the horrible drug from his former struggle in the Yellow City. The extreme pleasure turned his limbs numb. Made him stop caring. That opiate feeling of fake happiness. Once again, he valued himself above all and didn't care about anything or anybody. Even knowing deep down it was wrong. All he wanted was to remain motionless forever in that ocean of delight. But after a while, some of the awful withdrawal symptoms came as before. Starting with an uncontrollable urge to scratch himself. President Woke knew this and had intentions of brainwashing him now that his guard was down. Vic tried to piece together his thoughts knowing there was no Grunge to save him from that torment. Opportunely, there were still friends to help him through it.

— Vic! — Danny said with clear precision —. Don't speak or he'll find out. Just listen. I managed to hack into this frequency to let you know that we're here for you. And whatever Woke will employ as torture, summon all the strength within you to endure. You're much more powerful than he realizes.

— He's right — Pauline said moments later —. But that strength also comes from the people who love and believe in you. Don't forget us and you will be able to overcome any hardship that comes your way.

After hearing these encouraging words, Vic shed a tear that was washed away in his aquatic surroundings. It made him think that the supervillain was wrong. He couldn't control everybody. And his friends were proof of that.

As was the lesson with his former antagonists, Will was much stronger than lost love, mind control or pleasure. And no amounts of water could break the devotion he got from Danny and Pauline.

Vic glared at President Woke with rage while igniting his fire powers at full capacity. Even over his potential. Burning the pleasure and the withdrawal symptoms with pure determination. Heating up to 400%. Going from boiling water to bubbling magma. The clone underestimated the fact that the alien could do this in his own water park. For starters, he wiped out the greedy babies who would have probably sued him when they grew up. The lava then burst through the crystal, submerging the supervillain in his opposite. Melting away the Progressaurus fortress they were in. Vic managed to retrieve his Walkman and put on his headphones.

PLAY

President Woke fell from the melting PC Godzilla in a cascade of fire. After colliding face first on the burning lava below, Vic landed on his back to make sure he sunk completely. The villain made many attempts to use his water powers and counter the effects. But the heat was too much for him. So hot in fact, that Woke turned into steam. In the brief period Vic thought he was beaten, the vapor flew away unbridling an evil laugh. Apparently, it wasn't over. The alien needed to vanquish the evaporated version of his foe before he could condense into his former self. Luckily, the tampered water also exited the Red People as they woke up from their poisoned personas. Much like the Blue People did after Black Silence was defeated.

SOMETHING IN THE WAY

Vic streaked through the skies and followed the supervillain in a fiery blaze. The evaporated nihilist took many turns, changed speed and created mist to lose him. With the many obstacles in between, it made him think he could never truly be happy. Basically, because depression makes you see everything like an obstacle. Like something is always blocking your path. But, as a superhero, Vic was determined to catch him and was always on his tail.

President Woke crossed over to the Freemont district and turned to 36th street. There, underneath the bridge, was the Freemont Troll. As if giving it a soul, Woke entered the stone sculpture and made his half-body come to life. Vic landed in front of him and realized the supervillain was right. There's no beating water. A different approach was needed. The one the alien hated most of all.

STOP

— I'm gonna crush you now, varmint! — President Woke said smashing the ground with his wounded ego—. Yer gonna pay with your life! AND EVERYBODY ELSES!

— Wait — Vic said humorously evading the blow to one side —, there's something different about you... did you get a boob job?

— FIGHT, YOU COTTON PICKIN' YELLOWBELLY!

— I have a different proposal. Why not tell me a riddle? If I lose, I surrender myself to you. But if I give you the correct answer, you must turn yourself in.

— You think I'm that stupid?

— I don't know. Are you? You sure talk, act and look stupid. If you're unable to beat me in a game of riddles, then you're probably even stupider than I thought.

— I CAN DARN BEAT YOU AT ANYTHING!!!

— Prove it.

— I may could even beat you in trivia. Ask you when the I-90 mid-lake bulk was replaced.

— 1981. Sunk 1990. My father gave me a lot of meaningless info on Seattle. Maybe to know what type of perils I would face.

— You sure bout' that?

— C'mon! Give me a hard one.

— Say I beat you at yer own game. THE UNANSWERABLE QUESTION!!!

— What happens when an Unstoppable Force meets an Immovable Object?

— No, the other unanswerable question.

— You don't mean...

— YESSSS!!! OUT OF THEM BIG FOUR, WHO'S THE BEST GRUNGE BAND?

— That's more of a troll question than a riddle.

— I am a troll now, ain't I?

— That question really has no answer.

— In actuality, it has four right answers and four wrong answers. Only need one wrong'un to beat ya. Hint: 1) Pearl Jam ain't Grunge and too mainstream to be considered good, 2) Chris Cornell's voice ain't that great as y'all Grunge folk say it is, 3) Alice in Chains is dang monotonous and boring music for depressive junkies with a death wish and 4) Nirvana sucks, is overrated and ain't got no good songs aside from Smells Like Teen Spirit. RECKON I'LL LOVE WATCHING THIS HERE RIDDLE TEAR YOU APART!!!

— YOU REALLY ARE A TROLL!!! HOW CAN YOU SPEAK SUCH BLASPHEMIES! NONE OF IT IS TRUE!!! Unless...

— What? You forfeit, alien?

— No... I figured it out. You just gave me the answer, asshole.

— Fine, boy. Let's hear it.

— Four wrong answers. If I choose any band, I would be losing. Because none of them is better than the other. Four right answers. All of them are the best. Because the Grunge movement wouldn't have been the same by taking out one of the Big Four.

— Very good, varmint! — the troll said clapping sarcastically —. You won this here round. But ain't gonna keep my word. Thinkin' I rather stomp you into the ground!

— To be honest, Steamy... this whole riddle thing was a diversion. I only needed some time to heat the ground beneath you and keep the evaporation process going with no place for you to go.

— YOU DERN TRICKSTER!!! YOU SWINDLED ME!!!!

— Nope. Only smarter than the average troll.

PLAY

Vic continued to heat the magma from below while drying out the troll from within. President Woke's feeble attempt to escape as a light breeze human silhouette was later confined by the alien who threw his flannel shirt at his waist to trap him in flame shackles. Now his nihilism stayed like it should be... Endless, Nameless.

Pauline and Danny showed up a while later to hug him with joy. They assured him his rep was clean after the clone's indifference in confessing his evil plans and the absence of the tainted water in all Crystal citizens. Those who then founded a mutualist community among all identities without the separatist mentality provoked by Woke's false inclusion regime.

TAPE STOPPED

As he bid farewell to his friends, the Alternative Valkyrie hologram appeared once again bearing his mother's face. Performing his consistent Grunge ritual, Vic got on his knees and confessed his iniquities:

— Bless me Goddess, for I have sinned. I wanted to get Brody blackout drunk and dress him up like Freddy Mercury. Have a one-night stand with the Housewife from Hell. Run down the Holy Engineer with Ozzy's Crazy Train. Strap Devolutionizer down Clockwork Orange style and make him watch Bill Nye the Science Guy to see the innocent experimenting he never got. Wanted to put on a dress through the whole ordeal to fuck with all the homophobe accusing minds. I peed while in the Nevermind pool and felt the urge to castrate the Rednecks and the Rainbow Ninjas (before I knew they were water) just to see what they would believe in without balls.

Ending his prayers, a new note fell from the sky with the word "Kat" written on it. He found this one the most confusing. Why was cat spelled with a "K"? What did the four words mean all together? They made no sense. Maybe it was nothing. Only time would tell.

PART FIVE: THE VIC GRUNGE DEFENESTRATION

ENTER METAL MASTER

Vic awakened in his spacecraft as always. He looked around and smiled remembering having succeeded in his quest. Liked or not, the superhero beat the supervillain clones and helped everybody in Window World. But something else started to attract his attention. A voice. A very familiar voice from his past that was calling him. Maybe the happy ending that he was hoping for since it all began. And going outside, the earthling truly believed it to be so. It was his father. He was alive!!!

— Dad? — Vic said with illusions brewing from his radioactive chest.

— Hello, son — his dad said smiling—. It's been a long time.

— What are you doing here? I thought you were dead.

— I've always been here. Watching you become the hero you were meant to be. Couldn't be prouder.

— I think I'm missing something. Are you a spirit? A clone?

— No, I'm very much alive. And it's the original me.

— You've been here from the start?

— I have.

— Why speak to me until now?

— I couldn't reveal myself just yet. I did help you indirectly though. I connected your consciousness to the astral plane so you could see the ghosts that assisted you, I set up the J.P. Patches code, I gave Mister H the original altar artefacts for your Golem... not to mention the flannel shirts. Would you have been successful without them?

Vic looked at him with suspicion while reflecting on his words. His eyes lit up with an infernal anagnorisis after a minute.

— While we're on that subject— Vic finally spoke—, would I have been successful without the supervillains? It's too much of a coincidence that they were evil and you genetically engineered them. Something I imagine you expected from the beginning since the flannel shirts could imprison all the clones. Even setting them up to be unappreciated in their own cities and becoming what you always wanted them to be. Then there's the poppy fields and the Doom Orb paradox.

— Are you saying I staged all this? C'mon, son. What do you take me for?

— This will sound very Anti-Star Wars, but you're not my father. So, stop pretending to be. I hate clones. But I hate myself even more. Which makes me think that I'm a clone myself.

Vincent remained silent for a moment. He took out a small keychain with a button, pressed it and put it back in his pocket.

— You know what I really regret? — Vince said changing his paternal tone of voice to that of a villain—. Not making you dumber. But I suppose intellect was inevitable when combining the DNA of Eddie Vedder, Chris Cornell, Layne Staley and Kurt Cobain.

— So, why did you? — Vic asked somewhat happy to share in the famous rockstar gene pool.

— It was the only way I could truly triumph over Grunge music.

— Grunge music? What does Grunge have to do with anything?

— IT HAS EVERYTHING TO DO WITH IT!!! After creating this scenario, I called myself Metal Master after my band. The one Grunge destroyed.

— I don't get it. Was it Nu Metal? Thrash Metal? Doom Metal? Grunge complemented and never really erased any of these genres except maybe... NOOOOOOOO!

— Oh yes.

— GLAM METAL??!!

— You got it.

— But... Glam metal, Hair bands... they really, really suck!!!!

— SHUT THE FUCK UP!!! YOU DON'T KNOW!!!

— Know what? That you're a supervillain that's pissed because he can't dress up like a girl anymore?

— Try Nemesis. It's what I am to you. Because Grunge music was my own Nemesis. I started my band very young. As I said, I called it Metal Masters. My stage name was Vince Brawn. I was the frontman and played rhythm guitar. The rest of the band was great. We had a drummer who could play upside down in a cage, a bassist with incredible slapping skills and my brother who played lead guitar and had faster guitar solos than anybody in the business. I wasn't too bad myself. Learned all the chords to be learned and managed to have a long range in my vocal harmonies. We had a great run. Infinite pussy, drugs, money and fame. But we started too late. The 90's had begun and Grunge bands made a mockery of the Glam scene. I'm actually from Seattle so we were the first ones to fall. Nobody took us seriously anymore. I lost it all. Broke, women laughing in my face and even lost my brother to a drug overdose over the humiliation he felt. I swore I would get my revenge. Reason why I decided to focus all my energy on my scientific capabilities. Getting sober, for starters. Then selling my mansion and all I had left to get enough funding. For years I studied and became an expert in chemistry, nuclear physics, astrophysics, and most of all, genetic engineering. I spent years collecting the necessary genes for my master plan. Stalking your Grunge Gods from the beginning to create the perfect symbol to vanquish. I kept the name Metal Master to remember the shame. Keep myself motivated. I had to be on top again. But then... the planet was at its end. That part was true. And it completely ruined all my work. So, I turned to the stars to find a hospitable biosphere. Window World was the perfect place to start over.

— Ironically, an alien is going to kick your ass off this planet.

— Another twist for you is that you're not technically from Earth. I mean, you're DNA comes from humans and you're indeed an alien by pure genetic standards, but I made you right here. My planet was long gone when you woke up in Ground Zero for the first time. I travelled here eons ago and was put in cryogenic hibernation until recently.

— Still... the time tables don't add up judging by your age, your Glam Metal days, your scientific prep time and the advanced tech at your disposal. No way this happened in the 90's or early millennium.

— Very perceptive, Victor. I'm impressed. Judgement day occurred on April 5th, 2035. But there's an explanation for that too. Though Grunge was dead by the year 2000 and other Glam bands kept going, it didn't change the fact it ruined my life. Long before your first awakening, I engineered your memories. Downloaded a ton of general knowledge into your brain linked to experiences you never actually experienced. Even left some gaps and mixed specific symbols to generate a need for meaning. Ever wonder why you can't recall which part of the States are you from? How you remember doing the video from the beginning but the child in it wasn't even you? How you're Mom's memory is only linked to the nonexistent Melvins stories and you don't know the actual rock band? Or how you can remember other Grunge albums from the Big Four as well as other Rock labels and only remember fragments of the four albums you heard in Window World? Not to mention the fact these last four were chosen by you and yet associated to the zone of your destination. That was all me.

— None of it... none of my Earth memories are real?

— You had to believe you had a life back home. Back in the 90s. But you never did. You're nothing. And isn't not having a life and being a nobody the very definition of being a loser?

— I'm the loser? Need I remind you that I beat all your clones. Every supervillain you whipped up in your petri dish. So, you lost to Grunge once again, Metal Master.

— Did I? In truth, everything went according to plan. You see, my dear Grunge Rock Alien, in order to destroy a nobody, you must first make them a somebody. You're a hero to all the cities in Window World. If you had been the alien that arrived out of nowhere, historical publicity aside, nobody would have cared. You may think they never appreciated your efforts, but they do. Now it's time to turn the hero into a villain. Therein lies my victory.

— I'm not turning evil. Not for you or anyone. How pray tell are you going to do that?

— Easy. Making you explode. Killing all the people you saved. And not even your last neuron of intellect can save you this time.

— If I could withstand all the Hell I experienced throughout this whole ordeal and kept my emotions in check, what makes you think it will be any different now? I can take the grief and I'll beat you just the same.

— That's where you're wrong. I'm not like the antagonists you faced before. I'm your Nemesis, remember? There's not going to be a test, riddle or battle where you come out on top in the end. What was it you said before? Only Ozymandias got it right? I already triggered the bomb in your chest. It's set to go off any time now. Fact is, exploding before you beat everybody wouldn't have been as successful. But still would have served its purpose.

— MOTHERFUCKER!!! Are you so stupid that you don't see you'll die too????

— Wrong again. Both myself and the clones are immune to the bomb that will go off. Why do you think I let President Woke go ahead with his mad nuclear holocaust plan?

— And Feminazi's male extermination, Black Silence's mental manipulation and Mister H's world draining plans? I suppose they were orchestrated as well.

— Don't you get it? The Crystal People never mattered. They were a means to an end. I gave the clones freedom to fuck them up as they wished since I had already promised them so much more afterwards. They also have failsafes of their own if they even thought about betraying me. So, if they blamed me for their suffering, they knew I could exterminate and replicate them just as easily. Bottom line, only the Crystal People and yourself will perish. Once the planet is clear of all of you, a new dawn of humanity will awaken from the clones I harvested in secret. You might have seen some of them in all the cities. I also had to produce copies on the other side of the planet because I ran out of space. This new generation will know about your recorded good deeds and how you lost your mind to kill everybody. Grunge music will be associated with mass genocide and Glam Metal will reign supreme without any fucking interruptions.

— THIS IS NOT OVER!!! I'LL FIND A WAY BACK!!!

— I'm afraid not. Isn't it common sense that clones don't have an afterlife? Least of all you who don't share the immortality traits of the other clones. In a few seconds, you'll be nothing but dust. Bye-bye, Victor. Like I said, couldn't be prouder.

Metal Master's evil laugh echoed throughout the planet as Vic Grunge was about to explode. His chest glowed in different colors while his life flashed before his eyes. But they weren't good memories. It was the whole line of assholes he met throughout his time in Window World and some of the fake memories implanted by his false father. That which would trigger the explosion, killing himself and everybody on both sides of the planet... except the supervillains and the lesser clones about to be brainwashed by them.

THE FLANNEL REBIRTH

Evil had triumphed. Metal Master freed the supervillain clones and smelled victory in the radioactive air. Or so he thought. Because there were two loose ends that were not tied up in his master plan. First, the fact that the Sentinels could also withstand the nuclear explosion and survive the blast. Truth be told, the radiation was very mild due to the Crystal People's tendency to crack by just about anything. And the alien only died because it detonated in his own chest.

Then there was the other loose end: the Fifth Flannel Shirt. One that not only embodied the powers of all four elements, but also had the power to resuscitate the dead. And only the combination of Wind, Lightning, Earth and Fire could make it happen. Metal Master designed it in case Vic Grunge was needed again in the aftermath. This had to do with the fact that the alien's Nemesis no longer had the original rockstar DNA nor the means to replicate it. Even using Vic's blood, the resulting clone would be inferior as it was extracted from a copy instead of the original. Which was not the case with the supervillain clones whose stem cells were genetically engineered with immortal jellyfish DNA. Therefore, making them everlasting and easy to reproduce as identical clones.

Seen as servants to the city, Metal Master never considered the Sentinels a threat and underestimated the fact that they would side with his enemy. They were forced to listen to Grunge so their characters were more relatable to the alien and his 90s Earth culture. But this would also blow up in the supervillain's face. Since their motivation was the Grunge music they came to love and the hero that died to preserve it. Aside from the pain they felt losing the Crystal People they swore to protect as aliens themselves. Though familiar with Vincent Grunge, they had no idea about Vince Brawn and his ulterior motives. He had to be stopped. The four guardians only needed to steal the key from Metal Master's Hairy Fortress (literally a fortress with hair) atop each Mount Rainier replica in each of the four cities.

Every Sentinel handled the colored key of their own city. Since Metal Master didn't even take them into consideration, they had clearance to pass through security without restrictions of any kind. So, getting the four keys wasn't a problem for any of them. The issue was the flannel shirt itself that was hovering in a satellite that revolved around the square planet. Luckily, they all had abilities to achieve this; one that could create fuel from mud, one who could control plant life, one who could engineer technology from bones and one who could pilot the ship to its destiny. Hence the Spacecraft they created with their combined teamwork. Wood Goblin made the capsule out of a large tree, Bee filled it up with rocket fuel, Star Dog enabled the flight tech and Stone Pilot flew it to the satellite above.

The last Sentinel entered the space station. The shirt was locked up in a great glass case of reinforced Deaf Metal. The flannel was green in color and was glowing with mystical powers. Contrary to the other flannel shirts, this one wasn't bound to a specific zone and worked everywhere. In front, there were four keyholes color-coated to the cities and their respective keys. Stone Pilot introduced each one in the correct slot: purple, blue, yellow and red. Once turned, the glass case opened and Stone Pilot retrieved the mother of all flannels. He returned to the rocket and went back to Window World to reunite with the other Sentinels.

Coincidentally, Vic Grunge's corpse remained sizzled in the same spot where he blew up. Metal Master left him there after realizing there was no need for the reincarnation of his Nemesis after all. Another mistake that would come back to haunt him. And that moment came when the Sentinels dressed him in the green flannel where he stood as a hardened ash statue. The mystical effects of the garment soon regenerated his body piece by piece until it made him whole again. Vic Grunge came back from the dead and was now even more powerful than before. Though at first, the superhero appeared disoriented by the entire incident.

— Sentinels? — Vic said a bit light-headed and perplexed—. What are you doing here? What happened?

— You blew up — Wood Goblin answered—. That's what happened.

— The Crystal People?

— Gone...

— No... it can't be... I failed them. How is this possible? Why am I still alive?

— We brought you back to life with the flannel shirt you are wearing now.

— It can do that?

— Yep. It's sort of the flannel shirt of Life. It can revive the dead due to the fusion of all four elements synched to the entire Window World atmosphere.

— We're not really sure what its full potential is— Bee added—. Only that you can use all your former powers anywhere and are basically invincible. Keeping your memories intact. Though I'm positive Metal Master made the shirt with a failsafe. Even after erasing every memory of himself from your mind and starting over.

— Metal Master— Vic murmured in anger—, now I remember. I'M GONNA KILL HIM!

— Relax, tough guy — Stone Pilot intervened—. Since we're not sure what the failsafe is or what weapons they have, you're going to need all the help you can get.

— They? — Vic asked.

— Oh yeah, all your former villains are with him. Though we already predicted the wicked nature of most of the clones, your Nemesis surprised us as well. Never realized such an evil motherfucker was behind it all.

— That's just peachy... wait... you're coming with me?

— We didn't bring you back to life to talk about the fabulous Seattle weather — Star Dog said playfully.

— But I was a dick to all of you— Vic pointed out with remorse.

— Well, this is what real friends look like, bitch.

— Helping you in the bad times — Bee added.

— When you think you less deserve it— Wood Goblin retorted.

— Even if you tell them to stop dancing for no reason — Stone Pilot concluded crossing his arms—. And yet, they want to keep the party going. Together. Wherever that may be.

— Thanks, guys — Vic expressed in admiration—. It really means a lot you consider me a friend. I consider you friends as well. Still... Jeremy, Ray, Pauline, Danny... they were my friends too. Now they're gone... along with all those poor people... and it's all my fault. I feel like crying an ocean right now.

— Please don't— Bee said lacking the motivation to cheer him up—. Though you could. There's no longer a bomb in your chest.

— That's true! — Vic realized as he looked down.

— Fact remains— Wood Goblin stated—, you can either mope or do something about it.

— So, what's it gonna be? — Stone Pilot asked.

— LET'S TAKE THESE MOTHERFUCKERS DOWN!!!!! — Vic screamed with conviction.

— OH YEEEEEEEAH! — Star Dog prompted.

WHEN NATURE
SCREAMS

Vic and the Grunge Sentinels were now a team. An alliance that could face Metal Master and his evil quartet of Super-Clones. They went into the alien's spaceship to prep for the battle that lay ahead. Though Vic was ready to take them on, the Sentinels still had to work their magic. Literally since they had mystical powers that they could use against the supervillains. Star Dog was one of the key members at this point since his superpowers had to do with turning bones into advanced tech.

First, he created a Stinger Launcher for Bee out of femurs. It concentrated his mud honey making skills, creating solid stingers at will that were launched from his mouth. His regular stinger was covered in a green laser that could cut through steel. Second, he harnessed Wood Goblin's ability to control plant life in a ruby colored war suit made from craniums; even a skull helmet the sprite gladly sported. What this did was invert the source. Instead of controlling the nature around him, it could spawn the nature from within. Even when there was no flora to be found. For Stone Pilot, he used cartilage to fashion a military officer hat equipped with super sneakers. The shoes enhanced the visions that were projected while dancing and the hat could redirect them for mind control. Specifically, the ability to make his foes believe they are living in a different and more convincing reality. Now the subject could not question what was going on around him. Stone Pilot also accessorized some aviator sunglasses just for fashion. As for himself, Star Dog created a long range of fire weapons from different types of bones which included revolvers, pistols, machine guns, Uzis, bazookas as well as older weapons like crossbows, knives, shurikens, darts and swords. For ammo, he used teeth covered in the same laser tech as Bee's stinger which was also applied to the arrows and darts of the classic arsenal.

Prepped and ready to go, all of them marched out of the spaceship with Vic Grunge leading the way. Even without his 90's music, his mind, heart and soul could still hear it everywhere. It would be with him. Always.

While thinking on how to find his enemies, it turned out his enemies were already waiting for him outside. His lost love Feminazi was wearing a purple spandex two piece with a swastika in the center shaped like four Fs. Black Silence had on a dark bulky robotic suit with many shining blue lights. Mister H sported a steel yellow outfit with a helmet in the shape of a syringe. He also had long needles instead of fingernails. President Woke wore a hot tub suit where he could stay in his water form and was nearly invisible to the naked eye. When using his powers, hydro jets would make him glow red with the flowing water. As for his Nemesis Metal Master, he used a black Deaf Metal suit with the letters "MM" engraved in pink on his right pectoral. His hair was also pink with long poofy qualities and a pink star with glitter was drawn on his left eye.

— What do you know? — Metal Master said boastfully—. If it isn't the Grunge Rock pussies.

— We're the pussies, Clitoris Head? — Vic taunted him.

— This is what a man looks like, FYI. It was your music who fucked up everything. Including male fashion sense.

— Grunge had nothing to do with you wanting to look like a bitch.

— Well, soon we gonna make you our bitch— Black Silence spoke without resisting—. And all your little homeboys too.

— Did you really think we wouldn't find out about your betrayal? — Metal Master addressed the Sentinels.

— What can I tell you? — the big insect said indifferently—. When you underestimate a bee, you get your ass pinched. And not in the good way.

— Nicely put — Metal Master responded—. But short lived. You have no chance against us. So, might as well forfeit.

— Somebody is still underestimating — Star Dog said amusingly.

— No, I'm not. Because Grunge doesn't even exist. It's not a movement, it's not a genre... IT'S NOTHING! Which means you are all nothing and will become nothing!!!

— Did you hear that, Woke? — Stone Pilot commented with the same satire—. He's talking trash about Nothing. You better do something about it.

— I actually agree with him, varmint — the President responded with an evil water grin—. Nothing here I cain't never could wash away.

— I really hope somebody mixes you with soda and you die in your own puddle of greed, cocksucker — Wood Goblin added.

— I'm sick of this — Vic said seriously—. All this troll bullshit about Grunge not being anything. Anyone who says that is envious of its success or doesn't get Grunge at all. It's a way of life. A feeling of disconformity against a system in decadence liberated by distortion and lyrics of alienation that ironically make you belong to music itself. The word Grunge is an affiliation to those sentiments in the musical perspective of bands who, though not alike, are singing about the same thing. Different sounds that channel the same agony and turn it into something beautiful. But all that talk... Big Four bands are not the same, flannel is not a thing, only Alternative Rock exists as a genre, it's just a musical period, Grunge must come from Seattle... IT'S ALL BULLSHIT!!!!

— You gonna cry now, Vic? — Feminazi said mocking him.

— Not for you, sweetheart. My tears are reserved for things that matter.

— Honestly— Mister H said sarcastically—, I like Grunge. So many deaths claimed in my honor.

— There's nothing honorable about it — Vic responded—. If anything, their deaths made them stronger. Immortal. And the only real heroin in Grunge is the ability to take away the pain.

— Enough talk — Metal Master interrupted—. Your little speech won't mean shit in a while. Soon we will eliminate Grunge once and for all and Glam Metal will be the only musical genre.

— Wait, bitch — Black Silence whispered to his leader—. That's not what you told me.

— And a soundproof room for you, Black Silence.

— With occasional Trap Music, you know what I'm saying?

— Yes, you can listen to whatever the fuck you want!

— You damn right!

As the conversation ended, superheroes and villains lined up. Each Sentinel taking on the Clone leader of their city while Vic took on Metal Master himself. The villains attacked immediately and forced the heroes to take evasive action. Feminazi sprung SS laser blades from her wrists and started attacking Bee. Jumping and twirling into the air with a lot of skill until she put the insect to sleep with sonar tech. Black Silence generated a canon from his arm with noiseless waves that immobilized Wood Goblin completely. Mister H struck Star Dog with a golden-brown melodious ray that spawned from his needles and converged in one blow to weaken him. President Woke unleashed a strong water torrent against Stone Pilot. He could barely make a move. Let alone dance. As for Vic, the consequences were much worse.

— DOOM SUIT — Metal Master shouted—, PLAY GLAM METAL!!!

— So obvious — Vic said while falling weakened to his knees—, and still, I did not see that coming. This... music... it's just... horrible... even by Glam Metal standards.

— IT'S MY BAND, MOTHERFUCKER! THIS IS WHY YOU SHOULDN'T BE ALLOWED TO LIVE!

— Oh, this is Metal Masters? You truly suck balls then. Were you really rich and famous? I never heard of you before.

— You think I would implant my band in your memories to make you question and later sabotage my whole plan?

— And yet in the memories you implanted from the 80s, you remind me of the all-girl rock band Jem cartoon. Was that you?

— Hey! We had a good run with a decent fan base! And really hot groupies!!!

— Who probably thought "A cappella" was an Italian hat. Can't you play something more tolerable? Like Mötley Crüe?

— FUCK YOU.

— Alas, I will die a most terrible death.

— Funny you should mention that. This music will not only take away your powers and weaken you, but it will kill you gradually.

— No shit it's going to kill me. I'm not sure I'll be able to wait that long. I'd rather kill myself and die a second time than listen to this crap.

— NOW YOU REALLY PISSED ME OFF!!!!

Despite the Doom Orb's death sentence, Metal Master started beating Vic without mercy. Punching and kicking him until he coughed up blood. While enduring this on the ground, the alien glanced around him and saw his allies in a similar situation. Bee dozed off and snored with a deranged buzzing sound. Feminazi was prepared to deliver a final blow with her SS blades. Wood Goblin stood as if petrified like a statue while Black Silence approached him with confident steps. His advanced tech turned one of his arms into a chainsaw. Mister H had Star Dog on the brink of a drug overdose. Shooting his narcotic rays with a sadistic smile on his face. President Woke kept Stone Pilot floating in a water sphere while drowning him progressively. Metal Master finally stopped the beating, seeing his heroic Nemesis swollen and covered in blood. The supervillain smiled knowing the superhero was about to die.

— GRUNGE GANG! — Vic screamed in a wounded voice to his super friends—. THIS... DOESN'T LOOK GOOD. BUT... I DID FIGURE SOMETHING OUT. AS WE UPDGRADED OUR ABILITIES, THEY... DID THE SAME THING USING BLACK SILENCE TECH. AND OUT OF MY OWN... EXPERIENCE, THIS CAN BE INTERRUPTED WITH SOMETHING REALLY... NOISY. ANY... THOUGHTS?

— BZZZZZZZ — Bee snored.

— MRRRR — Wood Goblin murmured.

— GULP — Stone Pilot gargled.

— Great — Vic said to himself losing all hope.

— C'MON GUYS — Star Dog shouted in a wasted voice—. I KNOW YOU WALK VERY SLOWLY, BUT YOU SHOULD HAVE BEEN HERE BY NOW!!!

— IT'S OKAY, STAR DOG. AT LEAST WE TRIED...

— NOT TALKING TO YOU, VIC...

— THEN... WHO?

Star Dog slightly raised his head and smiled as he saw something in the distance.

— THEM!!!! — the Sentinel clarified.

Vic glimpsed in the same direction and saw a whole forest that wasn't there before. They appeared to be moving as well. After a while, he could distinguish they were the Screaming Trees from the underground Yellow City. They had joined the fight against evil. Fulfilling exactly what Vic asked for moments ago. A high pitch shriek that, combined as a chorus, took out all the Clone Tech as well as the Glam Metal music emanating from the Doom Suit. With this incident, Feminazi had no longer any lasers, Black Silence had no access to any of his noise paralyzing tech, Mister H could only administrate smaller heroin doses through tactile submission or short-range auras, President Woke's water supply was cut by half and Metal Master had no more restraints upon the green flannel shirt. However, the supervillain had another deterrent. Something that jeopardized his immediate plans. But he was not prepared to lose again. He held out his arm and pressed a pink button therein.

It was the new generation of clones. Stored in all the Seattle cities as well as the giant eggs on the other side of the planet. The ones thought to repopulate Window World. But they weren't ripe or human at all. They were freaks. Quadrupeds. Deformed monsters that obeyed only one Lord. The dark pink one deemed Metal Master. Synched up to destroy all who were considered unworthy. Controlling the masses as the god Poseidon would control waves in the ocean. And that's how it all went down. Making them swarm around the already weakened Grunge Gang like hyenas over a gazelle carcass. The superior clones slowly backed away and regrouped behind their leader.

THE CLONE
SHOWDOWN

Though all the heroes were discouraged by the giant army of clones, Vic still had high hopes to win and encouraged his Team to do the same. For starters, regenerating his own wounds with his Life powers and then proceeding to heal the rest of his party.

— Well — Stone Pilot said looking at the freakish quadrupeds running towards them—, now what?

— All of you handle whatever those things are — Vic said believing in his new flannel shirt—. I'll take on Metal Master and the Super-Clones.

— You're gonna take them out on your own? — Bee said impressed.

— Like you told me from the beginning, they're assholes. And kicking the shit out of people who don't give a shit is my thing. Besides, I already beat them before.

— Not all four— Wood Goblin emphasized—. With Metal Master leading them to boot. Not that I don't believe in you, dude. I just don't want to see you die again. Note the flannel revived you once. But I'm not sure if it will happen again or if the creator of the shirt can find a new way around it.

— Thanks for your concern — Vic said with his confidence unfettered—. But I must do this. It's been my purpose all along.

Only this time, I will show no mercy. All of them will die by my hand.

— If that's how you roll — Star Dog said hiding his own concern —. We'll try and keep these fuckers off your back. Fact is, NOW WE HAVE AN ARMY OF SCREAMING TREES ON OUR SIDE!!!

— YOU GODDAMN RIGHT! — one of the trees shouted.

Vic nodded with a thank you smirk. All the Sentinels nodded in appreciation as well. Though in their own minds, they wanted to help him fight the Super-Clones. And to achieve that, the freaks had to be taken out swiftly. Bee started regurgitating his mud honey on the inhuman clones. Entire groups were taken out while the ones left over were sliced by his laser stinger. Wood Goblin spawned vines that wrapped the freaks up and later cut them up with sharp rose spines. He also shot millions of splinters that hit the forehead of many quadrupeds. It killed them instantaneously. Star Dog was an all-out action hero, unloading ammo while yelling like a lunatic. First with the heavy guns, then worked himself down to the classic weapons. Stone Pilot started dancing and took the clones to another dimension where they saw each other as the enemy and ended up killing each other instead. The Screaming Trees continued their slow march while they shrieked supersonic waves that vaporized the hordes in an instant. Even though the Grunge Gang could stand their ground, the inferior clones appeared to be limitless. Springing from the soil itself and attacking in massive packs. There were even evil Nevermind babies! This left very little time for them to help their friend and leader, the Grunge Rock Alien.

While all this was happening, Vic faced his former foes and his Nemesis once again. His head slightly tilted, his eyes filled with rage, his fists hardened as rocks and a green aura surrounding him.

— I thought you were an idiot before — Metal Master scoffed—, but now you're just plain suicidal.

— Well— Vic said sincerely—, I am Bipolar. Being suicidal is another definition for being brave.

— You can't win, Vic — Feminazi said unsympathetically—. You care for me too much. Which means you'll fold. You're not a real man. And only a real man can beat a real woman.

— You're forgetting one thing— Vic responded—. I believe in phrases like, "I shot my love today."

— What about me, bitch? — Black Silence intervened—. You think you can beat me without music? You got no inspiration juice to go on.

— Grunge is a part of me now — Vic clarified—. All the music I need is playing in my head. Feeding my very soul. Not even Deaf Metal ear plugs will save your ass now, bitch.

— You really think that little soul of yours will help you this time? — Mister H added—. You'll be addicted to my unique charm before you can even make a move.

— Nope — Vic said confidently—. As it turns out, pleasure and responsibilities are two different things. And my need to do the right thing outweighs any possible blowback. Don't you know I just say "NO" to drugs now? Isn't that what beats any lowlife cockroach drug dealer?

— Not thinkin' straight, son — President Woke said with a sinister smile —. If I had my druthers, I S'wanee I'd kill y'all till you and yer friends are worn slap out into nothing.

— Really? — Vic answered sarcastically—. I always thought that anybody who believed in nothing would become nothing. No amount of water states will change what an inbred piece of shit you are.

— All your snappy comments won't change a fucking thing— Metal Master reiterated—. You'll lose because everything you believe in is for losers.

— Didn't all this mind fuck of a story come to be because you're a sore loser and are making up for your spoiled brat denial? — Vic pointed out—. I'm sick of everybody telling me I'm going to lose. Giving up is what makes you a loser. And I'm not backing off. SO LET'S DANCE, MOTHERFUCKERS!

Without even a warning, the Four Clones attacked him simultaneously. Feminazi increased her pheromones until generating a love ray to confuse his feelings for her whilst being magnified by Mister H and his opiate aura. On top of this, Black Silence joined in with plasma beams shot from his palms. As Vic fell to his knees once again, President Woke started to drown him in a water torrent. But the alien resisted. He started summoning his flannel strength while shielding the attacks with his left arm. Vic's whole facial expressions turned psycho. Moments later, all his harnessed power deflected the attacks to their origin with his right hand. The Four Clones were launched ten feet back, seeing how the Grunge Rock Alien was still standing and sneering with fury.

As they didn't give him the honorable courtesy of waiting, Vic hastily attacked Feminazi turning his flannel purple with Wind powers. This time, there was no holding back. Even defending herself from the alien's fast attacks, she was caught completely off guard. Particularly when Vic threw Feminazi into a tornado that launched her into the air and kept her spinning until she fell wounded to the ground. His Ex was beaten. She couldn't stand a chance and was well aware of it. But like any proud Nazi that could not accept defeat, she swallowed a cyanide pill and died. It was there, seeing her dead, without superpowers and all enchantments vanishing in the air, that he knew he really loved her.

Vic tried to contain his feelings about it by immediately assaulting his next foe. He jumped on Black Silence who wasn't as keen as Feminazi in martial arts. With his flannel glowing blue and even faster lightning punches, Black Silence couldn't even fight back. Getting crushed as fast as he could breathe. But the villain soon retaliated with his lesser tech. Specifically, mechanical arms from his spine that grabbed the hero by the waist trying to rip him apart. Realizing there was little time, Vic grabbed both sides of the supervillain's head with his palms and delivered a high-voltage electric shock that fried his brain into the afterlife.

As he stood victorious in front of Black Silence's corpse, a wave of joy filled his veins. False happiness. A feeling that was well known to him. Pleasure spiked with pain. Without even realizing it, Mister H had him in a heroin headlock. The Super Dealer even jacked up the amount. Vic resisted all he could and summoned his yellow flannel with all his might. A sharp obsidian rock spawned from the ground between them, breaking off both the villain's arms with blood squirting from his shoulders. Vic then created many geode fists in a hyper-combo that ended with the villain laying on the ground beaten to a pulp. Vic finished the job by summoning stakes from the ground that killed him in a way no painkiller could ever heal.

The Grunge Rock Alien turned now to President Woke and his seemingly indestructible Water powers. Though the Screaming Tree attack damaged the recycling capabilities of the hot tub suit and reduced the liquid available after each skirmish, the clone was still as sturdy as he was in the Red City encounter. The villain continued to spring floods and large containment bubbles against him. This only slowed him down, but Vic was so determined to end it all, that it didn't take him long to be free of the short-term water restraints. He turned his flannel red and started punching him like the others. But this time, his Fire punches only resulted in steam that barely tickled the President. The superhero thought about using his lightning powers again but there was a chance electricity would only make him stronger. So, it was more practical to go back to the basics. The way the supervillain was beaten before. But much more gruesome. Vic literally dived into his stomach as if it was a swimming pool. Carefully adjusting his entire body to smoke form as to enter his suit without breaking it. And from the inside, he increased his internal temperature until generating magma. The lava consumed the villain inside out who gurgled himself into nonexistence. Being consumed from within the enclosed hot tub suit where there was no mist or breeze form to escape as. Only the nothingness Woke faithfully believed in.

THE HIDDEN TRACK

As Vic was beating the Super-Clones, the Sentinels continued their everlasting fight against the humanoids. Bee sliced through with additional laser stingers and subsequent mud honey bombs, Wood Goblin continued to use plant life to cut, maim and poison, Star Dog unleashed all his war arsenal to tear them to shreds and Stone Pilot kept dancing to create confusing scenarios that would lead them to their own demise. Not to mention the aid given by the Screaming Trees who vaporized all the freaks with every screech. They eventually killed them all and regrouped to assist their Grunge leader. Metal Master noticed he was outnumbered. But there was still one more song in his Glam Metal playlist.

— It's over, Metal Master — Vic stated while sensing his reinforcements walking his way—. Every woman in Fat Con has fucking sung.

— Why is it over? — Metal Master rebutted while multiplying himself into an army that quadruplicated the heroes—. If it's related to numbers, IT'S OVER FOR YOU!

— Jesus Christ... deny your maker.

— That's right, you piece of shit. You really thought I wouldn't apply the clone technology to myself?

— Overcompensating, are we? Replication won't change the fact you have pink Glam Metal pubes surrounding your micro-penis.

— I'M MORE OF A MAN THAT YOU'LL EVER BE!

— But wasn't this a trial of manhood? So far, I've seen you hide behind your Doom Suit music, Super-Clones, Monster-Clones and now... Identical-Clones? Are you not man enough to face me on your own?

— Oh, don't worry. My other selves are to keep your friends occupied. YOU AND I ARE GOING TO FINISH THIS ONCE AND FOR ALL!

— GAME ON, POODLE-FUCKER!

Vic turned to his team and nodded as if giving the order to fight the Metal Master clones. They all understood and continued their struggle for Grunge Glory. The original Metal Master then started to hover and an ominous rumble broke in the air every time he moved. Vic flew towards him in an offensive thrust and attacked in a continuous manner. His flannel turned purple, blue, yellow and red as he applied punch combos of Wind, Lightning, Earth and Fire. Metal Master defended all his bouts with minimal effort, shielding each blow with one hand while having the other resting on his back. Little did the alien know that the hidden hand was even more deadly. It countered an innocent punch that launched Vic thirty feet from the strike. He suffered additional injuries with the ground, rocks and plant life. Though giving up was not an option.

For the second round, Vic flew back and stopped at a distance. He decided to use elemental powers instead of brute force. First, a whirlwind in purple, then a lightning bolt in blue, followed by a giant boulder in yellow and concluding with a hail of fire in red. Metal Master absorbed all the attacks through his Deaf Metal suit and then proceeded to merge the same powers in one powerful one. This translated into a colossal fireball thrown at lightning speed with an intense sandstorm covering its tracks. A blow impossible to defend. Which resulted in the Grunge Rock Alien taking the lethal hit and reducing his life span by half.

Metal Master didn't stop there. He moved swiftly with his horror movie sound and started to punch and kick him from all angles. Vic took all the blows. Coughing up blood again. There was no strength left in his body. Nor the skill to beat him. The superhero clone underestimated his Maker. Though at the same time, Vic couldn't believe he could be that good. As if his Nemesis already knew the outcome. Metal Master identified which combos would be thrown before he identified them himself. Was he from the future? Was it the clone DNA programming? Or had it something to do with the incredibly strong musky scent that came from his suit? His green flannel and his Life powers could identify this odor as pure testosterone. Though everything felt confusing, there was a way around it by unravelling the mystery. Something that was easy to do with the stereotypical supervillain pride fueled by man juice.

— You... really stink — Vic said in his weakened and injured state—. I mean... literally. Like skunk junk... deep-fried-in-melted-gorgonzola stink. Can I interest you in some Teen Spirit deodorant?

— Funny you can't recognize the smell — Metal Master answered boastfully—. It's the scent of a real man. A Glam Metal Rocker! Just as your deceased lady love was genetically engineered to exert pheromones, my Deaf Metal suit oozes testosterone. Optimizing my every move. Which is why I can know everything you're going to do before you do it. Combined with Black Silence tech, H's painkiller regeneration and Woke's water-based malleability, I'm virtually indestructible.

— So, your weakness... is for me to turn you into a pussy.

— Perhaps. But at the speed I'm emanating my male essence, it's impossible for you to do so.

— I'll find... a way...

— Like your friends? You were so busy focusing on me you never realized there were twenty versions of myself doing the exact same thing to each of your beloved Sentinels. Have you even looked back?

Vic turned around and was shocked to see his friends dead and mutilated. Including the trees were reduced to sawdust. All the Metal Master clones were standing around them laughing. Vic shouted with all his pain as he realized his failure. At the same time, all the testosterone taunts made him understand something. The Alternative Valkyrie and the seemingly meaningless messages received in each city. Vic noticed that the riddles he hated so much were the very thing that would save him.

— By the way — Metal Master said preparing a glowing and deadly karate chop—, the green flannel revival was a one-time thing. Though I could kill you repeatedly with extreme pleasure, I think two times will suffice. Any last words, you Grunge fuck?

— Yeah — Vic said smiling and slowly healing in secret—. How's about four, asshole? SANDOVAL... LOUISE... DONITA... BJELLAND!

— Hmm... okay. Explain.

— The Alternative Valkyrie. Well, Valkyries really. I figured out the riddle. I needed to fill in the gaps... to summon them.

Metal Master laughed and replied:

— You're so naive that you're basically retarded. There are no Alternative Valkyries. Another made-up incentive to keep you believing in something. I sculpted four statues for you to pray and projected them in holograms. Even made them look like your fictitious mother to encourage you. Nothing more.

— And the four words given to me... after each prayer? — Vic insisted.

— What the fuck are you talking about? There are no words or riddles. Aside from being an idiot, you're undeniably insane.

— Actually... it's faith, motherfucker. The hidden track. When you believe in music... it shows up again unexpectantly. It becomes alive.

That's why even if you beat me... Grunge will always come back to kick you in the nads. You can kill me... the Sentinels... vanish us from the mortal plain. But historically, we will always show up again and again and again.

— Really? And where are your Alternative Valkyries now?

— You mean those two women behind you?

Metal Master turned around and saw that his Nemesis wasn't lying. There were two women approaching in winged horses. They were dressed in Uru armor and were swinging bone steel flails. And it was none other than Louise Post and Hope Sandoval.

— So what? — Metal Master grinned with indifference —. Women crave the very ground I walk on.

— That's just the thing — Vic clarified—. These are not groupies. It's pure Riot Grrrl, bitch. Not only are you about to face women who won't bow down to you, but you're also about to get beaten up by girls. Isn't that like... the opposite of testosterone?

— I doubt those cute faces can pack a punch.

— They can. But they're really distracting you from the assault of the punkier cute ones.

— What?

Before Metal Master could figure out what his words meant, two other Valkyries appeared from behind smashing his balls with Morningstar maces. It was Donita Sparks and Kat Bjelland. Hope and Louise arrived shortly after to continue the beating. They clobbered him for a while then proceeded to take out the already weakened Metal Master clones. While all this was happening, Vic used the green properties of the flannel to heal himself while indirectly reviving the Sentinels. Not exactly bringing them back to life, but instead synchronizing their ghostly figures to the realm of the living. This use of power consumed Vic's age and turned him forty-three years old in an instant. As if choreographed in their method of thinking, each Sentinel drew an ecto-boombox and raised it on top of their head harnessing alternative rock melodies. Bee would provide the drums, Wood Goblin the bass, Star Dog the rhythm guitar and Stone Pilot the lead guitar. The only ones without a boombox were the Screaming Trees who, also revived by the alien as ghosts, started screaming Grunge style.

PLAY, PLAY, PLAY, PLAY

Vic smirked at the deteriorated supervillain and his testosterone-free suit. He unleashed all his elemental might, mixing fire punches with windy roundhouse kicks, lightning elbows with earth headbutts and ending it with an elemental ball as the one used against him. Except a lot bigger. Much more concentrated. A giant metal boulder bursting with lava surrounded by a cyclone of magnetic shockwaves.

— IMPOSSIBLE!!!! — Metal Master yelled looking at the giant elemental ball—. I CAN'T LOSE AGAIN! NOT TO YOU! I GAVE YOU LIFE! WHAT THE FUCK ARE YOU GONNA DO WITHOUT ME??!!

— ONLY WHAT YOU TOLD ME TO DO, POP — Vic screamed over the magical noise and music—. KEEP GRUNGE ALIVE!

— NOOOOOO!

Vic released his final attack. In his depleted state, Metal Master was unable to defend himself against it. Not even with all the combined attributes harnessed from the other clones. It blew him away into nothing. Dead as Glam Metal. The Grunge Rock Alien emerged victorious and joined the Sentinel Ghosts on the ground. The Alternative Valkyries flew down in their winged horses shortly after.

STOP, STOP, STOP, STOP

— Well — Vic said happily—, we did it. Couldn't have done it without any of you.

— You needed us— Louise said—, so we came.

— On that note, where did you come from? Metal Master himself said it was all a hoax.

— You already know— Hope answered—. We came from you. I mean we died back on Earth, but your faith made us exist by calling out our names in the astral plane. As did the Hall of Fame. The afterlife for our kind.

— You mean "Valhalla of Fame" — Vic said playfully.

— Yeah — Kat confessed—, that does sound better.

— Badass too — Donita added.

— So, you guys— Stone Pilot said to the other Sentinels—, let's go christen our new crib!

— You got it! — Wood Goblin shouted.

— Most definitely— Bee remarked.

— Party in Valhalla of Fame tonight, madafakas! — Star Dog screeched.

— I'll be running a little late — Vic said with somewhat dark humor—. I must revive the Crystal People first.

The group went quiet for a while and looked at each other in disbelief.

— Are you fucking kidding me? — the Valkyrie Sparks spoke—. Bringing your friends back consumed half your lifespan! And they're just ghosts in the existing realm like us.

— Reviving the Crystal People will definitely kill you — the Valkyrie Post added.

— That's what I meant when I said I would be running late— Vic reiterated.

— Don't do it — the Valkyrie Sandoval confirmed —. You have lost so much already. It's not fair to you.

— And being suicidal about it isn't helping either — the Valkyrie Bjelland reprimanded—. Do I have to remind you they were assholes?

Vic lowered his head in silence as if reflecting about what they all commented. Moments after, the alien looked at them and said:

— I know the risks. And it's not because I'm suicidal. Suicide implies I'm doing it for selfish reasons. And I'm not. I'm a hero. I have to do it. The Sentinels would agree with me on this. Even if they're assholes, I have to believe that they're not. That being one has to do with the ones in power feeding them lies and bullshit so they become proud and stupid. I would rather die knowing that I saved them, than live realizing they weren't even given the chance. It was never about the man I was supposed to be. But the man I was going to be remembered as. What purpose is there to live without you or them? That would be truly selfish. Not to mention sad. I don't see it as a win. Only a daily reminder that I failed. My death will bring them life and they're memory will make me immortal. Isn't that what the meaning of life is all about?

Another moment of silence washed through the Rock personalities. The Sentinels understood from the beginning, but hid their sentiments about it. Though they hated to see their friend die, what he said made all the sense in the world.

— So — Star Dog said finally—, Valhalla of Fame?

— Does the Window World Pope shit in the woods? — Vic said humorously—. NO OFFENSE, SCREAMING TREES.

— DIDN'T HEAR YOU — one of the trees shouted—. BUT NONE TAKEN!

— Hey I do take offense to that! — Wood Goblin said joking —. It's heavy shit!

— Pope? — Bee pondered about the joke—. Like a Prosperity Gospel?

— More like songs from the Vatican gift shop, bitch! — Stone Pilot added.

The Alternative Valkyries all had a half smile and somewhat of a glow of admiration in their eyes. They bowed their heads in silence. Vic responded the same way and turned around shortly after. He kneeled and put his hands flat on the ground. His flannel shirt started to glow as did the soil he leaned on. It quickly spread throughout Window World bringing both the cities and the inhabitants back from the dead. Including the Crystal Baddies he personally had killed. As this was happening, the Grunge Rock Alien started to age quickly until turning into dust himself. From his ashes sprung Alice who later joined the Sentinels, the Screaming Trees, the Melvins, the Lees, G.A.C.V. and the 27 Club celebrities who tagged along for the afterlife celebration. The Valkyries proceeded to lead them all into the Valhalla of Fame leaving behind the memory of Vic Grunge.

Though the Crystal People did not know of his sacrifice at first, they eventually found out on both sides of the planet. Thanks to the Valkyries and Sentinels who could move between life and death, Grunge music started to surface as a divine omen in apparitions, scientific evidence and folklore. Thus, perpetuating his image far beyond the grave. Soon everybody would acknowledge his greatness. Their superhero. Their savior. Their Messiah.

The Grunge Rock Alien.

THE END

BIBLIOGRAPHY

Https://drive.google.com/file/d/1hvpo63payMP5zTxj8PzWT-nstVGYcpdE/view?usp=drive_link

Also by Cronos Carpio

Grunge Rock Alien